JO BA

*Much love to
my friend
[signature]*

LONG ROAD THROUGH THE FOREST

outskirts
press

Outskirts Press, Inc.
http://www.outskirtspress.com

ISBN: 978-1-9772-2691-4

Cover Image by Jo Barney

Outskirts Press and the "OP" logo are trademarks belonging to Outskirts Press, Inc.

PRINTED IN THE UNITED STATES OF AMERICA

1

GERALD

Jake told him he was nuts to go looking for an old woman who hadn't cared enough to ever find out about him or his mother and was probably senile by now and wouldn't remember anything about anything. "You're looking for a decrepit old crone and for what reason? You think she'll somehow help you? Give you something? She never cared before, did she? Jake held a blunt between his fingers and, inhaled, and closed his eyes. "Stupid. She won't now either when you knock on her door and ask her to take you in. Like usual." Reluctant smoke poured out of his nose and mingled with the smell of rotting garbage. "No one's going to care about you except maybe me, you know."

Moon pulled himself upright, wrapped the damp army blanket around his legs, and looked out over the tents and the lumps of huddled bodies scattered across the camp. Traffic rumbled as it crossed the vibrating overpass above them. Oregon mist glittered in the streetlights. Several fires flickered across the camp, probably not cooking food, just warming up a few square feet of concrete. Campers had used newspapers as mattresses, blankets from the agencies to hide under as they slept. Tents, small, blue, red, yellow, huddled along the edges of the camp. Plastic bags overflowed with garbage that barricaded the border between the street and the sleepers. The uniformed clean-up squads supposed to toss the bags into a garbage trucks hadn't been around for a while. Neither had the guy, nervous hands in his overcoat pockets, who posed one time for cameras in front of the truck. Someone said he was the mayor. Moon wouldn't know. He just wished the camp didn't smell so bad.

His stomach churned as he breathed in Jake's smoke and he turned his back to it. Jake said he missed him, even when he went to jail and left Moon alone for weeks. But Jake was stingy with his caring. He cared mostly about his drugs, his cardboard space and orange tent and pack stuffed with supplies, and finally, Moon's body, which offered pleasure and income. Sometimes, Jake said he was glad that Moon shared a tent. Maybe like right now. Moon felt a hand squeeze his limp penis. Then Jake's weight pressed down on him, Jake's voice became a furious painful growl.

When Moon woke up he felt a wet lump on his cheek and he might be bleeding. One eye wouldn't open, his jaw crunched when he gritted his teeth. A quilt lay heavy on his body. And then he remembered.

Jake, high, angry the way meth made him, screamed that Moon had stolen his stash, hit him so hard Moon had fallen backward, his head landing on something hard. He heard someone say, "This is not good," and Moon felt himself being lifted to his feet. "This is what makes us all seem like criminals."

A man, gray beard curling against his neck, had led Moon to a tent. He gave Moon a wet cloth to wipe the blood off his head, told him to lie down until morning. The man whispered that he was leaving with his cart to collect bottles; he'd be back, not to worry. He would return to help a good boy like him get out of such a bad place like this one. "There's a whole world out there, young man" he added, and Moon could see a slash of lips smiling at him. When Moon was sure his rescuer was gone, he pushed his way through the old man's tent flaps, found his pack under a pile of blankets in Jake's camp, and headed out between the line of plastic bags, his feet sliding as they struck the street's wet asphalt. He would look for a mission someone had told him about, the Green Door, on Oak Street.

The tired-looking woman, gray circles puffing under her eyes, pushed her black-framed glasses higher on her nose as she said, "Welcome." She directed Moon to a chair. "I'm Grace. What can we do for you?"

Moon wasn't sure how to answer. *Make my eye stop hurting? Find me a bed? A toothbrush?* "I need. . . everything." As the words escaped, he wiped a sleeve across his cheek, but the scratches and bruise hurt and he let the tears drop onto his jacket. When Grace asked again, he answered that his name was Moonlight Smith and that he needed a place to stay. The woman said, "A huh," wrote something down, made a phone call and in a few minutes told Moon that she had found a bed for him, and a shower and a meal, for one night in a teenage shelter. Tomorrow she would try to find a more permanent spot for him in a nearby youth refuge. "Might be a little difficult," she warned. "A lot of kids out on the streets this time of year, but I'll try. You look like you need a good night's sleep and a safe place to hunker for a while." She handed a form and a pencil to Moon and asked him to fill it out, as much as he could.

Moon hesitated at the first blank line. Name. Should he give his real name? No. He became Moonlight Smith the night he ran out on his mother who had passed out on the bed in that motel. Three months ago. He had hoped that the full moon lighting sidewalk in front of him meant good luck. Moonlight seemed a hopeful name that night. His mother probably wasn't even alive by now and his real name didn't matter anymore. He wrote Moon Smith on the line, no address, no family, and in the space asking for his drug use, he wrote "None, not anymore." He checked a few of the boxes next to a list: tooth brush, soap, shampoo, razor, laundry soap, comb.

Grace looked over the paper. "You're fifteen? Anything else?" Moon didn't know if the woman was asking about the blank lines for home address, social security number, and parents' names or the unchecked boxes for needed items.

He hesitated. "I maybe need to see a doctor" He touched his jaw, probably black and blue by now. "Do you have doctors here?"

"Medical van. Comes tomorrow. You can visit it in the morning. In the meantime, here's your pass for the evening meal and your bed number. Your dorm room has five other guys in it. Bunks." She pointed to the stairs at the end of the hall. "Room 7. And, before I forget," she added, "you have an appointment at 3:15 this afternoon to talk to Elena, our counselor—about those bruises and whatever else comes up."

Moon took the slip of paper Grace handed him, looked at it, then tossed it on the desk. "I don't believe in counselors. I'm not going." Grace folded the paper, offered it again. "If you want to stay here, have a meal, you have to talk to Elena. It's a rule."

"I don't believe in rules either." Moon stood up, slung his pack over his shoulder, bumped through the office doorway, made his way past the kids lounging in the lobby. Grace didn't try to stop him. Out on the sidewalk and into the smell of the food carts at the curb, he slowed down to rub the neck of his t-shirt across his eyes, careful not to press on the bruise. He wished he had a buck for a taco.

An hour later he threw up into the toilet of the men's lavatory at the county library. He cleaned himself up as good as he could at the sink, dabbing at his mouth, his sore cheek, and his leaking eyes. He felt a little better, but he looked terrible. The bruised cheek, the eyes, and it was impossible to pass his fingers through his tangled hair to calm it down. He still had a comb in his pack, he was sure. He hadn't left it behind with Jake, had he? He couldn't stand the thought of Jake giving it to the next kid he brought into his sleeping bag. Jake himself wouldn't need it. He'd shaved his head almost bald. "Nits" he had explained. "Besides bald is in now."

Moon sent his fingers deeper into the bag, felt the comb, dragged it out, but he couldn't make it dig through the tangles either.

"You have lovely hair," a ragged voice whispered. "A beautiful red-gold. Bountiful hair." In the mirror, Moonlight watched a gnarled hand reach out and pat the curly wad gathered at the top of his head. He turned. An old man, his eyes rimmed in mascara, his wrinkled lips glowing with bright pink lipstick, was squinting at him. Rouge trailed across the old guy's cheeks and onto ear-ringed ears. Coal black hair framed his mask of a face. "You need a little help to get it into some sort of order, dear. I can help." Cigarette-yellow teeth grinned at him. "I'm Richard. I am, well, used to be, of course, a hairdresser. I've seen hair a lot worse condition than yours in my day. Can't do much about the bruises. Maybe camouflage 'em. Come, sit down."

Moon glanced around. "In there?"

"Where else? We'll clean it up when we're done." Richard dragged a small suitcase across the tile and nudged Moon towards the only stall, its door gaping. "Hurry before someone comes. People get so pushy when they have to go."

Moon inched himself onto the toilet seat, closed his eyes.

Minutes later, Richard had clipped out most of out the mats. He brushed and combed and poured shampoo from a large bottle onto Moon's scalp. Crooked fingers pressed and moved through soapy piles of hair. No water? It didn't seem to matter. Moon tried to remember when he'd ever been touched so gently. The fingers continued to move as the old man hummed.

Then Richard picked up his bag and moved to a sink. He pushed aside a man drying his hands, stuffed paper towels into a drain and ran the water until it became warm. "Boy, come here," he called to Moon who still sat on a toilet, his eyes stinging, rivulets of suds dripping down onto his shoulders. "Now, water." Moon leaned over the sink, and Richard's hands swiped small mountains of soap into the bowl.

"God, now what? They're taking over. First, it's the benches, now it's the restrooms." A man huffed his way out the door. "I'm just not coming downtown any more. This is ridiculous. A normal person can't even. . ." His voice faded away as Richard ran more water into the sink, rinsed Moon's hair until strands of it squeaked when he pulled on them. Then he led the dripping head to the blasting hand dryer. After a few moments he said, "There. Coiffeur for a prince."

At first Moon didn't want to look in the mirror. When he raised his eyes, he saw that he was wearing a spikey red crown. He grinned at the mirror. "I do feel like Prince Valiant. Sort of."

"Just keep them in control. A little water when you wake up. Those curls want to escape. Let me dab a little Cover Girl on your cheeks."

"Richard, I don't have any money."

"A thank you will do." The pink cheeks crinkled as he laughed. "I was young once, and handsome, believe it or not. Now I sleep in a mission along with a lot of other old has-beens. But I remember the good times—when I was lively, had a boyfriend, a couple of them, a mother who loved me no matter what." He touched Moon's arm, a touch even more tender than the others he had given in the past half hour. His suitcase under his arm, Richard turned to leave. "If you have a mother, maybe you should go back, see how she is?"

2

ALICIA

I pull my sweater up around my neck. One of the many disadvantages of being old is that I am often chilly despite the thermostat set at 72 degrees, a level I live in both day and night. Probably the pinging of the hard rain on the window is making me feel cold. I close my book. I should lower the shade. That's when I hear the sound. I push against the arm of the sofa and take a deep breath, rise up. My slippers shush across the carpet, as I edge toward the window. The rain rattles both the panes and my sense of balance. I catch the shade's cord and tug at it.

In the narrow band of lamplight leaking out into the yard, I see a shadow--a stirring--then the shadow melts into the dark. I lower the shade. The doors are locked. Years ago, Fred taught me to lock up at night and I always do.

The thought of tea quiets my breathing. A cup of green tea will send me to bed ready to finish Penelope Lively's novel.

As I push through the swinging pantry door, I hear the knock. Not a loud, insistent sound that shakes the air, but a pathetic murmur so unsure of itself that knuckles have only brushed the surface. Surely not a gang member or a psychopath, I think, only someone lost, maybe afraid of intruding, needing directions or a phone to call AAA.

I go to the entry, squint through the peek hole, and see two shadowed eyes looking back at me, eyes that appear to be waiting, not frightening.

Fred advises, *Don't open the door.*

I turn the lock, open the door six inches, push my hip against its edge, one hand ready to slam it shut if necessary, and say, "Yes?"

A voice, hesitant, slides out from beneath the edge of a hood. It whispers, "Hello, Grandma."

"Who are you?" I haven't talked for days, and my throat is dry. I open the door a few inches wider.

The hood falls back onto a shoulder. A spray of red hair springs up. "I'm Moon. My mom said if I ever got in big trouble, I should come to you, Grandma."

I step back, ease the space between us.

For Godsake, Fred warns. *Shut the door.*

The boy's jacket shimmers with rain. His shoes, wet, muddy, have tracked the porch. The sight of his wild, anxious hair sends a prickle of fear down my spine and I close the door, lean against it. Someone has played a trick on this vagabond, has sent him to my house on a foolish mission. Doesn't the NO SOLICITORS sign mean everyone, including a grimy teenager who wants something from me?

Words leak through the mail slot. "For just a minute? To dry off. Then I'll go."

The soft rap of knuckles again. Then, "Grandma?"

I have no granddaughters, grandsons, any kind of children. And only a ghost of a husband.

Dull thuds vibrate against my shoulder as the knocks continue. I hear his voice again. "Please. I need to talk to you. That's all I need, nothing else."

A pathetic note rings like a knell in the boy's words, makes my fingers turn the knob.

Ignoring my good sense and Fred, I whisper, "Come in, whoever you are, but drop your things right here in the entry. Your jacket, also." I cannot remember when I last invited a stranger into my home. Never a wet, dirty one. I've been warned about opening my door like this by the AARP magazine and the *Oregonian.*

And by my resident ghost.

In the last year or so, I have not even invited in people I know. In my old age, I have come to appreciate the precious solitude of my days. This pathetic voice on a rainy night has invaded my very precious peace.

Don't say I didn't tell you, Fred warns, drifting away.

I wait until the boy sheds his shoes, coat, and sodden backpack on the entry carpet, an ancient Persian that had dealt with years of Fred's wet galoshes. Then I lead him into the back of the house, to the kitchen, and point at the stools at the counter. He glances at the cupboards, at the dishes drying in a rack. He shakes his head and wet pricks of red hair send droplets of rain onto the drain board. I haven't much to offer him. In the bins of the fridge is a bag of asparagus that I, in a weak moment, had intended for a brunch I chose at the last minute to not to go to. "Oh, Alicia, the hostess had lamented, we haven't seen you for so long. Don't disappoint us." But I did. I have nothing in common with the neighboring housewives whose interminable conversations center on grandbabies and demented husbands and new knees.

"Asparagus?" I ask.

"I love asparagus, I'm vegetarian. . . sometimes."

I take out the day-old whole-wheat muffins I had planned for breakfast, a pot of cream cheese, and the jar of dried up jam. "Not gluten-free, I'm assuming?" Beggars can't be choosers, I almost add. "Since you somehow think you know me, I need to ask your name."

"Moon. And no. I just try not to eat anything with eyes." He sends a hesitant smile in my direction as he combs his fingers through his wet hair. "Mostly." He is ruddy from the cold, bruised on one cheek, his eyes blue, very blue. Beginnings of a mustache shadow above his lip. He seems small for his age, fourteen, fifteen maybe.

I open the bag, jar, container. Why I am about to feed someone who doesn't eat things with eyes, why I have invited this person into my kitchen, why do my hands shake as I dig into the cream cheese with a knife and spread the bread with thick layers of something that may have had eyes. "Does milk from a cow fit into that description?" I ask. Impossible to know the rules anymore.

"Nope." He reaches for the saucer holding my offering. "Sometimes eyes don't count. When you are hungry. A week ago, I ate a few grasshoppers, soaked in soy sauce, barbecued over a campfire." At my gasp, he smiles, "They were good, crunchy, salty. . ."

"Grasshoppers?" I let loose a disbelieving "Shit," a word I save for special occasions. Something about the fiery hair, the bright eyes squinting at the muffin he holds to his mouth, the white teeth, straight except for one incisor that stands out in protest from the others. Something about him is touchingly vulnerable.

Careful, dear. He may be a serial killer. Fred is back, cautious, worried.

"I have tea. Do you drink tea?"

Not waiting for an answer, I set the kettle on the burner. "Earl Gray? Or mint?" I take the mint tea packet from the box. Vegetarian probably means no caffeine.

"Do you have coffee, maybe instant coffee?"

I've guessed wrong. "I have this glass thing and some coffee. One of my caffeinated neighbors brought it to me a long time ago because tea gave her a stomachache." I set the contraption on the counter, pour a tablespoon of coffee grounds into it, along with a cup of boiling water, and push down the handle. This is more cooking than I have done for anyone in months. I calm my shaking cup and saucer as I carry my tea to the table.

"Bodum."

"What?"

"That's what they are called." The boy points at the small pot. "French."

He reaches across the counter and pours the steaming coffee into the mug I've taken out of the cupboard. "My mother had one." He is slim, boney, if I can judge by the thin wrist reaching for the chair across from me. When he raises his cup, I see the dirt under his nails and then, even more disconcerting, the ring of brown and gray staining his shirt collar. His hair, close-up, looks like wiry red moss.

"Does your mother know you need a bath as well as a cup of coffee?"

Despite the rudeness of my question, he looks back at me over the edge of his cup. "My mother is probably dead. In fact, I'm sure she is." He bites into the last crust of bread, washes it down with a swallow of coffee and adds, "That's why I am here."

"What's this nonsense about?" He is now crunching on a raw asparagus stalk and apparently doesn't hear my question. "Don't look away. I want an answer."

The boy, his name a strange one, picks at the muffin crumbs on his plate. He seems to be trying to decide whether to eat or talk. Then he lifts his head, his lips twitch into a small smile. "You're my grandmother. My mother told me that if I ever needed help, I should find you."

"Your mother? That's impossible. I have no children. Until you, I've never even had a child alone with me in this house. Who is your mother? Her name? And while we are at it, what is your name, really?" I try to keep my voice from wavering. Is this some sort of old peoples' scam?

He has put down his glass. His blue gaze captures mine. "My mother is, or was, Jessie Grayson, at least at first. She got married a couple of times when I was little and her name changed. I know about the Grayson part because that's always been my name. Grayson, Gerald Grayson. Until a few months ago when I became Moonlight Smith." His steady eyes challenge me. "I like my new name."

"A person can't go around changing his name whenever he wants to, like shoes. You are Gerald. The other name makes you sound like a 70's hippy and I've had enough of that nonsense in my lifetime. Besides, you must think about your school records, your social security number, the fact that your mother may be looking for you. "

"She's not."

"And your father?"

"I don't remember him." And before I can say anything else, he continues, "None of the others were my father either."

I don't want to think what "others" means. How many? What on earth was Gerald's mother thinking as she dallied, a toddler hanging onto her skirts? What kind of child emerges from a life like that? I look at the boy hunched across from me. His fingers move to his cheek. He winces. A good-looking kid, really, under the bruises and grime. If he was cleaned up, he'd probably do better making it through the city bureaucracy that deals with homeless children. Tomorrow I will call the CSD, initials I recall from some newspaper story about abused children. But first things first. "Gerald, would you like to take a shower?"

His grin answers my question. As he stands up, gathers his pack, he says, "I haven't been called Gerald lately. Since I was a kid."

And what are you now? I want to ask, but instead I take him by the arm and lead him to the bathroom next to the guest room.

Alicia, be careful, for Godsake. Fred again.

Well, why not? A good night's sleep before I send a harmless lost soul on his way.

"Leave your pack in that bedroom and I'll get you some towels."

The two of us meet at the bathroom door, and I hand him the towels, a tube of toothpaste, and a bottle of body wash. "I also have a tooth brush. Just got one from my dentist, brand new." Why do I feel so pleased to be able to offer a toothbrush? To a stranger who claims we are somehow connected? I go back to the kitchen to pick up the dishes and don't allow myself any more questions. I know they will come when I try to sleep a few hours from now.

When Gerald emerges from the steamy bathroom, wrapped in a towel, he says, "The best day of my life. A shower and a grandma."

His words land like lead weights in my stomach. I will shut the door I opened to this unsettling person in the morning. For now, I show him where the washer is and how to run it and I leave him unloading his bag and stuffing almost everything in it into the machine. We'll have to stay awake until it is time to put his things in the dryer. One night, I decide.

"What do you like on TV?" I hand him the TV guide from the *Oregonian*. If he suggests something with full of sex or loud music, I'll say no. I prefer old films and most often tune to the Turner station: Cary Grant, Olivia de Havilland or Barbara Stanwyck, comforting, sometimes funny films, about personal conflicts that are solvable, a little sex, yes, but not much grappling. I dislike the grappling of legs and arms and breasts and the other parts of the body that seems necessary to tell a love story these days. I don't remember sex being like that, back when Fred and I made love.

Gerald, searching the guide, may be reading my mind. "Let's see what's on. I like old movies. How about *Pulp Fiction*? Really old. And famous."

I have never heard of it and the boy's "old" turns out to be at least a generation away from my "old." No singing in Swiss meadows, no dancing in Paris in this one. I close my eyes during a frantic grappling session and then leave the room. "Why would anyone watch something so violent and loud?" He doesn't answer. "Want some coffee?" I call from the kitchen. Again, he doesn't answer.

An hour later, I gather the dried clothes and lead Gerald to the guest room, switch on the lamp, dump the armload on the bed. "Fold up your things."

"You didn't like the film, did you? Sorry." I turn to leave and he adds, "Can I leave the light on?"

This boy who enjoys violent movies is afraid of the dark. So am I sometimes. At least we have that in common. "Of course. Do you want a magazine or two to read before you go to sleep?"

"I just need to have the light on.'

"We'll figure out in the morning what we'll do next." The "we" that has crept into that promise surprises me. I close the door and spend a few moments wondering what is happening to me. "We?" I haven't thought in terms of *we* for years.

Watch it, Fred warns.

3

GERALD

Gerald began to fold his clothes, glad to see that his underpants had come out almost clean. The crotches didn't smell anymore and the gunk was gone. But peeing still hurt and he itched like crazy. He probably should go to a clinic or something.

Then he lay back and sank into a white pillow. He didn't pull up the covers because he was sweating a lot. Here he was in a real bed for once, but he was starting to feel sick to his stomach again. He closed his eyes, tried to make the itching go away. Something was wrong with him. Had been for days, seemed like. He drifted towards sleep, remembering the medical van that Grace had told him about. At the teen mission. In the morning. As he turned over, trying to cool off, he decided to sneak out early and not bother his grandmother with any more problems. *Pulp Fiction* almost gave the old woman a heart attack. No telling what a pack of groaning street kids at the medical van would do to her.

He woke up to a knock on the door. His grandmother brought in coffee and another muffin on a tray and she settled herself on the bed. "I've decided two things," she announced. "First, for the short time we will be together, I want you to call me Alicia, not grandmother or Mrs. Drummond. Both those relationships are moot."

Gerald could tell what 'moot' meant from the sound of the word. Alicia was a nice name, a little different from what he first expected, but close enough.

"And second, I will take you to Children's Services today and we will find you a proper place to stay. They must have foster homes for young people like you where you will be safe and well-fed." She moved the tray closer to Gerald, pointed to the muffin. "You liked these last night. Coffee, too. From the Bodum." She pushed herself up from the bed. "Good, your clothes are folded and packed. I'll get the toothpaste and brush from the bathroom. You can take them with you."

"Wait. . . Alicia. I don't . . ." and at that moment Gerald found himself leaning over the edge of the mattress and up-chucking.

"Oh! No!" Alicia hurried out and brought back a towel. "What a mess." She tossed the stained pillow to the floor. "Something you ate? Not the muffin from last night, certainly. What else?" She blotted the front of the t-shirt Gerald had slept in.

Gerald reached for the towel and vomited again. Then he sank back exhausted onto the bed and felt her hand on his forehead. "You're burning hot!"

"I'm really sick. My stomach." He didn't want to make more of mess than he'd already made, so he tightened up until the sensation passed. "I think I need to get to the medical van." He swallowed whatever was still trying to come up. "At Green Door. Maybe I can take a bus..."

"Bus! You must be joking. Vomiting all over strangers? I don't know what Green Door is or where it is, but I do know my own doctor. Get some clothes on. I'll take you to him." Alicia left the room, her lips pressed tight against her teeth as if she could close off her nostrils that way. The smell was bad. Gerald pushed his legs over the edge of the bed and tried to stand up. He was through throwing up for a while, he guessed, but he was so weak he could barely pull on his clean jeans and a different t-shirt. His hands looked weird. Spots on them. Spots on them. What next? He wondered. Measles? Do measles make you yellow?

"Measles?" Alicia looked at his face. "Not yellow, I'm sure. How would I know?"

"Just saying." Gerald tried to smile as if he wasn't worried. He didn't tell her about the weird shit coming out of him or the headache he'd had for at least a day.

Alicia dialed the phone in her hand and after five rings a voice answered.

"I have sick child here and it might be serious. He is very sick, hot, vomiting. . . What? I can't bring him into your office? This is ridiculous. The boy's s sick! He's a doctor. Isn't that what he does, heal people? Let me talk to Dr. Herring. . ." After a moment, Alicia disconnected and said, "You have to go to an emergency room. You may have something contagious, not fit for a doctor's waiting room full of people. You have any idea where the closest emergency room is?"

"Not around here, but I was in one once, at a hospital when my mom. . . Or you could call 911."

"And cause a commotion in the neighborhood? They'd think I'd died, like they did when Mr. Masuko was carried away by an ambulance and never came back. Only he didn't die, just went to his son's home. They looked for him in the obituaries for weeks. Get in the car. I'll comb my hair later."

The red-lettered sign led them to the entry of the Emergency section of Good Samaritan Hospital. When Alicia mentioned the fever, the two of them were rushed to a room off to one side where a woman behind a desk determined that the patient did not have insurance. "He's not mine," Alicia said when clerk looked at her. "I hardly know him."

That is true, Gerald thought, she hardly knows me, but I know I am hers, whether she admits it or not. Then the air dimmed. His knees buckled, he heard voices calling for a gurney. He was wheeled away.

When he woke up, he was in a hospital bed. A tube dripped something red into his left elbow, a white sheet lay heavy on his legs. Another tube sprouted from the top of his right hand.

"Just about finished with the transfusion," a voice informed him. "Precautionary. Your blood pressure was all over the place." A nurse, her pink smock alive with laughing pigs, reached up to adjust a knob on the tall stand holding several bags above her patient's head. "You'll feel better in a while." The pigs made Gerald feel better already.

A movement at the window caught his attention. Alicia, lit by pale sunlight under a partially lowered shade, turned the pages of a magazine, her straight white hair now combed, tucked behind her ears. "Glad to see you are coming out of it."

"What is wrong with me?"

"The doctor will explain when he comes on his round in a couple of hours. He understands better than I about these things."

"Am I dying?"

"No."

Alicia went back to her magazine and Gerald closed his eyes. That was good news at least. Not dying. He had another thought. "Did I have an STD?"

"I'm not sure what you mean. But the doctor said something like that." Alicia closed her magazine, stood up, her face stiff, her voice cool. "I am guessing, however, from your question that you are blaming this illness on sex. I don't want to know about it." She walked to the door, called over her shoulder, "I brought your backpack in case you need whatever's in it. I'll pick you up when they release you. In a couple of days."

Gerald had time to think about his situation: no money, an aching body, an illness that wasn't deadly, a grandmother who denies she's a grandmother, a dead mother who swore that Alice Drummond was her birth mother. She could prove it, his mother said in one of her sane moments, but she forgot to say how. All Gerald could look forward to after this safe, crisp bed was a cardboard mattress and more bruises and abuse from a person who'd just as soon beat him up as fuck him when he was high.

"Hey, can someone turn on the TV in here?" he asked another smocked woman, this time bobbing with daisies, pushing a cart outside his door. May be *Pulp Fiction* would be on Ted Turner.

The doctor, he had to be the head doctor since he led a white-coated parade in, said hello and introduced his interns who would be listening to his diagnosis and his talk with him. "This is the way doctors learn," Dr. Anoud explained when he saw the look on Gerald's face ". . . a normal procedure in a teaching hospital," he assured him. He opened his file.

Gerald wanted to listen, too, since he hadn't been told what was wrong with him, and he tried to ignore the six pairs of eyes staring at him. He wished he had been able to at least brush his teeth. His mouth tasted like he was half dead and maybe he was. He'd know soon.

Dr. Anoud looked at his folder and said, "Presenting symptoms are a sore throat, fatigue, headache, and what brought him in here, vomiting and a rash on the soles of his feet and palms."

The other observers, two women and three guys all nodded.

The doctor took Gerald's hand and turned it over. The rash was still there.

The five almost doctors leaned in, looked.

"Dr. Johansen," the head doctor asked, "please feel for lymph nodes in Gerald's neck."

A gentle finger pressed. A wobbly pain. She knew where the lymph nodes were.

Gerald wished she could also find his sore throat and fix it. Right next to the lymph node.

"You are observing the secondary stage. If left untreated, this patient will go into the latent stage and then into the tertiary stage, the spreading of the disease beyond the genital area. The brain, nervous system, heart, perhaps. Joints and muscles become pain-ful. If left untreated, it can lead to death."

I'm really sick. Gerald was not able to think beyond wanting to scratch the itch in his butt. "So," he finally managed to mumble through his painful throat. "What's wrong with me?"

"You have syphilis, complicated by a dash of hepatitis B." The interns looked at each other, shuffled papers in their hands. The doctor wasn't finished. "If your grandmother hadn't brought you in when she saw the rash on your yellowed hands, you might never have known until it was too late for us do anything."

Gerald was only a little surprised by the diagnosis. He'd heard about it in the camp, one guy whose face was dissolving, clap Jake called it. "That's why I give you condoms, whether you like them or not." He was talking to his "team." Gerald had just joined the team, was about to learn to play the game.

"A while ago you contracted a bad STD. Maybe the oldest in the world, but still with us. Often the symptoms are overlooked until they spread to other parts of the body, in your case, the rash.

"So, what should I do?"

"You should not have unprotected sex, for one thing. Right now, you are being fed heavy duty antibiotics to fight the infection that may be is spreading to other organs of your body. However, we believe that schedule of antibiotics and bedrest and regular blood tests will clear your symptoms, including the anal itch."

The group churned out of the room as the doctor paused and his thumb and finger gave the nurse an okay sign. "Good job catching that little glitch, the yellow skin. The shot and a little rest will take care of the hepatitis B."

"That's the first doctor who's said that to me," the nurse told Gerald after the room had cleared. "Thanks for recovering on my shift."

"How did he know I was brought in by my grandmother?"

"Someone in the ER noted that on your admittance papers. Maybe she told them. You were kind of out of it, I hear."

Had Alicia said she was my grandmother? After denying it? Why?

"If she isn't, she probably knew that we need to know your relationship to get permission to do certain procedures. She'd also probably mentioned responsibility for payment of bills. She was making it easier for you."

"So how long will I be here?"

"Until your nodes and sore throat check out okay. The rash is getting better and your color too." She leaned over him, adjusted a pillow, whispered, "Babe, you need to take care of yourself. Maybe not do what you've been doing." She touched his cheek, patted it. "You'll be out of here in a couple of days."

He pretended he didn't hear her advice. "That's a long time. Can I have control of the TV remote?"

"We'll be helping you sleep, but sure, you have at it until we fill the bed next to you."

It was very nice, being drugged up, in a cool bed and watching old movies all afternoon. About the time his dinner was brought in, though, a gurney was also wheeled in and on it a body, with dark stringy hair, and judging by the size of the mound of blanket over it, the fat arm covering a head, a big person. Nurses and aides got it onto the bed, closed the curtain between them, and when they had finished doing whatever they had been doing to it, they left.

Moans slunk under the curtain, mingled with the evening's news, the only program Gerald could get right then on the TV.

"Too loud," came from under the curtain.

"Sorry," Gerald called and turned the volume down and then off. If he were very sick, he wouldn't like the noise either. He wished he had a magazine, though, and he saw the one Alicia had been reading on the chair next to the bed. If he stretched out his left arm he could reach it. He rolled over and reached toward it. An alarm rang. Moments later, a smocked woman hurried in.

"Bad boy," the aide scolded as she stopped the leaking and reconnected the transfusion equipment. "You pulled the IV out. But we're just about finished with this. What were you doing and why didn't you call me? I'm Shirley, on duty for the next few hours."

"I needed something to read and I didn't call because I don't know how."

Shirley showed him the call button and handed him the magazine. "You met your roommate yet? We don't usually mix sexes in these rooms, but she got the last bed in this section." She grabbed a piece of curtain and pulled it back. "Hi, Peggy. Time to make friends. This is Gerald."

"Fuck you," Peggy said.

"I feel just the same, Peggy," Gerald answered. "Pretend this never happened and that this helpful person never touched our curtain. I'll read my magazine and ignore you."

"Asshole."

"Being sick doesn't give you the right to be mean, Peggy." Shirley closed the curtain and backed toward the door, waving goodbye at Gerald.

He tried to let his roommate know that he also was weirded out by this situation. "It's okay, Peggy. I feel mean too. Maybe we can be mean together—or at each other, which ever works out best."

"Shit. Shut up."

Gerald opened the magazine, a copy of something called *More* and everyone in it was at least female and at least fifty, but he had begun an article on Jane Fonda, amazing boobs, when the silence in the room shattered.

"I wanted that baby! I didn't care if it was damaged. Damn, **I'm** damaged. I would have been a great mother, a really great mother, better than my own mother that's for sure, and now my baby's gone. I tried to hide her. I'm so fat no one would have noticed until too late, but no, they made me take this test and they said she was all mixed up, parts of her missing, would probably die before she could be born, even. For sure after."

Gerald could hear Peggy gasping, her words a long pain-choked moan. "What do they know? I would have taken care of her, loved her. Oh, God, why are you punishing me? Sure, I did drugs, I'm not denying it, but not after I found out she was in me. I was careful after that."

Gerald didn't move, afraid that a sound from his side of the curtain would get the misery going again. But he guessed it would be terrible to feel a baby growing inside of you and have it taken away. A piece of you. A dream of you. He wondered if it would it be worse to have that dream born and discover it is damaged, without important parts, and then have it die? Like his second grade friend, Lila,'s mother, who had a baby born without a brain. That might be worse. Especially if you felt it was your fault, if you'd taken a drug of some sort at exactly the wrong time and kept part of the baby from growing. And you held the damage in your arms for a second and had to give it up. Lila said her mother went crazy for a while. Lila had too.

"It's not your fault, Peggy. It's God's fault for making drugs that kill people, make them need them. Not your fault."

"That's crap, boy. Shut up and let me die."

"Don't die, Peggy. You have lots of chances for a little kid to grow in you."

"I said shut up, whoever you are. God doesn't like you and neither do I. I'm going to sleep."

Jessie had told him about God's responsibility in creating drugs, the time she overdosed and he had called 911 and thought his mother was dead. He was nine and he had stayed alone in the apartment for three days and waited for his mother to come back. She did and she went to AA after that and got sober. For the first time in a long time, Gerald could expect dinner every night, and he and his mother did the dishes together, and only the weekends were lonely because his mother worked all Saturdays and Sundays at a restaurant. But she sometimes brought food home and the two of them ate supper watching SNL until he fell asleep. Then one Saturday his mother didn't come home. Or Sunday. Or Monday. When he came in from school on Tuesday, his mother was lying on the couch, her eyes closed. "I lost my job. We have to move." They moved, from then on, every few months, sometimes with a man, sometimes after a man, always with a plastic bag of colored pills hidden in the bottom of his mother's purse. Sometime during that time, it had become God's fault.

4

ALICIA

That's what I get for falling for a pathetic story from a pathetic child. A dash of joy, a bucket of misery, a mess to clean up.

When I get home from the hospital, I see that the mail has come. Requests for money, as usual. I leave the envelopes on the coffee table, except for the one that displays a nickel in the envelope's cellophane window. I pry the nickel out, put it in my pocket. Silly, those charities giving a nickel and expecting hundreds of dollars in return. Of course, nickels aren't worth much these days. Not like when I was six and lived down the street from Mr. Parson's Five and Dime, with the penny candy in a glass case in its front aisle, the better to capture kids, as their mothers wandered into other aisles.

I pour myself a cup of leftover tea and warm it in the microwave. A muffin, the last one, beckons and I take my snack to the sunroom and settle into my favorite chair, very good chintz, not the cheap kind that Meier and Frank's fabric department used to sell. Old but still colorful. So is the footstool. Just right for the sunroom. I prop up my feet and tuck a pillow under my bad knee. I'll probably need a new knee one of these years, but not right now. The cortisone shots have taken care of most of the pain, and I don't look forward to living alone and trying to manage the aftermath of an operation with no help.

My sick mother had hired a nurse to live in her house for the three years before she died because by then I was working and couldn't take care of her. At least that's what I told her when she asked to move in with us, but the reality was that I just couldn't imagine living with her any more. That was long ago, and I force my thoughts in a different direction now by closing my eyes and breathing five times very deeply, letting the breath out in whooshes, as my yoga teacher taught me when I used to go to yoga, before I got too shaky to get into a triangle pose without falling over. I still can breathe, though, and I send a deep inhalation in the direction of my knee. Sometimes thinking like that helps.

Whooshing doesn't slow rampaging thoughts, though. What is an STD? That's what the doctor called whatever had made Gerald sick. Something distasteful, I'm sure. I can think of one person, a moved-away neighbor, who might know. Agnes has grandchildren, six of them, their pictures bursting out of her pocketbook whenever we have had an occasional lunch out. She also has a computer that she claims knows everything. I reach for the phone and dial her number.

"Google says it means Sexually Transmitted Diseases," Agnes reads, her computer chirping.

"Like what? I caught mumps after Fred and I had relations. That's not so unusual."

"No, diseases that people don't talk about. Like gonorrhea and syphilis and a kind of hepatitis, and others I don't recognize. Why are you asking about this? Something you aren't telling me?" Agnes snickers. "No, seriously, Alicia," she adds, her voice signaling a more helpful curiosity. "Why?"

I can't think of an excuse, so I tell the truth, that a runaway boy came to my door, asking for help, and it turns out he needed to go to the hospital. STDs, the doctor said. I didn't know what that meant, something about having sex. "Syphilis, for example," he said. I have vague memories of horror stories about syphilis, about melting brains. "And other viruses." At least it wasn't AIDs. I am familiar with that disease. That's why I asked Agnes to ask her computer.

"And the boy?"

"He's still in the hospital for a day or so. Then he's out of my life. I'm too old for this kind of agitation."

"Well, good for you for helping a lost soul. Syphilis isn't fun, I've heard. Did I tell you my granddaughter got accepted at Reed? Of course, this means we'll all have to help with the tuition, me specifically. My kids think I've got money hidden away. Not that I don't, but. . ."

Agnes would have kept going, but I cut her off. "Have to go see how he's doing. Now that I know what he's got." I hang up and re- member that it was the doctor who mentioned the letters STD and syphilis. This is a fifteen-year-old boy who shouldn't know anything about them. He's just a kid. I won't call Agnes again. That woman enjoys too much the one-upmanship of having a Google.

I have two days to decide what to do about to this strang- er I have allowed into my life. I have no responsibility for him once the bill at the hospital has been straightened out. Maybe Obamacare will be good for something, and if not, I will be pay- ing the bill to get him to leave. A glass of wine will unstress me, help me think. Damn knee. I hobble a step or two until I can straighten my leg. In the kitchen, I open a bottle of Sauvignon Blanc and pour myself a glass. After a sip or two I begin to feel the slow return of the peace I had been in which I had been immersed before that soft knock at the door, the peace I have worked for twenty years to create.

A little music, Fred suggests.

I go back to the sunroom, place a record on one of Fred's old turntables, glad I have never packed this one away. Dave Brubeck filters through the sunlight. Dave Brubeck is a bad choice. He takes me on a down escalator into my dark storm cellar, a place I haven't gone willingly for years, dragged there only by my memories of certain anniversaries, our wedding day, our trips to San Francisco, our big 70's party in 1992 to celebrate our twenty-fifth anniversary, where Brubeck and MJQ, music from our San Francisco pasts, filled the room even though disco might have been more danceable, Fred sick by then and not dancing much. I've managed to put all that away somewhere. What good is it? Remembering makes me sad and then angry like I'm feeling at this moment.

Fred had been a thoughtful husband. He remembered birthdays and my choices of perfume and liquor, and he earned enough to keep us very well. This brick house, an English cottage with its fruitwood woodwork and arched windows, set amidst similar Portland homes built in the flush 1920's, was our last splurge before he died twenty years ago. Not because of the HIV, it turned out, which he had under some sort of control, but a bad heart that no one suspected. San Francisco business trips and the City's allure, had a hand in his death, but his arteries even more so, this man with whom I had never had children, and after a while, rarely touched. Early on, I suspected that he faked his relieved moans, maybe because he disliked the whole bed scene with me. I should have guessed about this secret side of Fred, should have spoken up, would, of course, have tried to change him, but I, dissatisfied, had created my own secrets. So, we lived in this lovely house, talking about everything except the truths that snuggled uneasily in the pockets of our lives. It was not a bad marriage. Just not a fully formed one. But it seemed enough at the time.

I shouldn't have put on the jazz. I'm too upset about Gerald, who claims to be my grandson and who almost died this week, to spend time looking backward. I changed to Chopin. No memories here, except that of my last recital when I played a shaky rendition of Valse in C sharp Minor. Or maybe E sharp Minor. Doesn't matter. After that recital, I quit lessons and concentrated on being popular in high school, which didn't go much better than the Chopin.

When the phone rings I almost do not answer it, my concerns about Gerald displaced by older events. I don't get many calls. Nowadays people email when they want to connect with someone, and I'm told I should get a computer or at least a fist-sized brain that one can hold in her hand and talk to and it talks back. Murial Wilcock, a lifelong one-up-some-ship person, demonstrated hers at a book club meeting I was coerced into attending a few months ago, and a female voice answered every question we had for her except for "Why can't I open the bathroom door?" which Susan had been yelling from down the hall.

"You have to shove it with your shoulder," the hostess called.

"My newly repaired shoulder, are you kidding?" Susan answered and someone went to rescue her before she needed another new shoulder. The digitalized voice apologized for not being able to find the needed information. The book clubbers all had another glass of wine, especially me.

I pick up the phone. I'm at least advanced enough to have caller identification, and I see that the hospital is calling. Gerald informs me that he is going to be released in the morning and he asks what he should do? "Some of my stuff is at your house. I don't know how to get there."

"I'll pick you up, of course. I'll want to talk to some people. I'll come at 11:00."

Hooked again. But I can't leave him standing on a corner, can I?

You might consider it at least, Fred suggests.

The papers for his release aren't ready, of course, when I arrive at Gerald's room. He is lying on the bed, dressed in jeans and a T shirt, his back pack on the floor beside her. When I come in, he turns off the TV.

"Can I leave now?"

"Papers still have to be signed. I've taken care of the bill. We're at their mercy now. We wait." I sink into the chair next to the bed and am glad to see the magazine still there.

As I pick it up, a voice rumbles from the other side of the curtain. "Why'd you turn it off? I was watching it, shithead."

I hold my tongue, reluctant to risk words in the presence what seems to be a very angry person.

"That's Peggy, my roommate. She's not happy, but she's getting better, I think. She lets me watch TV and even watches it herself sometimes. I should have asked her." Gerald raises his voice. "Sorry, Peggy. Here's the remote. Watch what you want. I'll be leaving soon." The remote passes under the curtain and I hear a grumbled "Thanks."

When the TV's sound comes on again, I ask, "Who is she?"

"Peggy. The doctors and her mom made her have an abortion. She really wanted that baby."

"How could anyone, in this day and age, force someone to have an abortion?"

"They convinced her that the baby would be born dead or would die soon. They gave her pictures of it in her stomach that showed that it was all deformed and they warned her that she herself might also die because of something happening inside her. Peggy said she'd not mind dying if her baby girl could live." Gerald lowered his voice. "And her mother said, 'Yeah, and who would take care of it. Not me, sweetie. I have enough on my plate with your psychotic brother.' So, she finally agreed."

"I hear you whispering, you rotten scab. This is my business, not yours."

Silence follows a frightening grate of a sob and the sound of the remote landing on the floor. Gerald slides off his bed and pulls the curtain to one side. I get up, follow him. What is he going to do? Assault this foul-mouthed abusive Peggy person?

I watch as he climbs onto the neighboring bed and lies down next to a large mound of a body. His arm stretches across what is probably a chest, his hand, a bandage still attached to it, touches a round cheek. Gerald mouths a NO as I move closer. He shushes and begins whispering a song. "Bah, Bah, Black sheep, Have you any wool? Yes sir, Yes sir, three bags full. One for my master and one for you and one for the little girl who used to live down the lane." The big girl's ragged lips move, silently repeating the words. Gerald sings the lullaby four times. By the last "Little girl," Peggy seems asleep and I need to wipe my eyes.

"She likes that," Gerald whispers. "My mother used to sing it to me when I was unhappy." He slips off the bed and looks at the door. "I guess it's time to go." A woman in a printed smock stands there, her hands on a wheel chair.

The aide glances at the two of us, one smiling, one in tears. "Which of you goes in this?" she asks, checking her paper, pushing the wheel chair forward. "The young one, says here." When Gerald seems about to object, she adds, "Hospital rules."

"I don't like rules." Gerald sits down and lets himself be rolled down the corridor.

"I didn't use to either," I answer, reaching for a tissue from the box on the bed table. "But they do make life simpler."

On the ride to the house, neither of us says much. Gerald is probably wondering where he'll end up next. I am wondering, too. I'm not willing to get close to a kid who has just been treated for two STD's. Or even one.

I think about rules. I have lived by well-defined rules They involved keeping a clean, attractive house with the help of a woman who didn't mind scrubbing out toilets, developing cooking skills that would allow me to entertain my husband's business acquaintances and wives, and becoming a somewhat important partner in the pipe manufacturing company in which I had begun as a temporary. Habits, along with rules, did make decisions easier. We made the bed every morning. I read the *New York Times*, every Sunday. We watched NPR news and local newscasts to keep up on things. We always had season tickets to the plays at a local theatre. That's how we avoided the fault in our marriage lingering like a toxic cloud over us.

However, none of these old rules and habits matter now, except maybe the bed making. During the past twenty years since Fred died I have shed most of them. I don't cook much anymore. *The New York Times* is a sometimes thing, bought at the coffee shop if I happen to get out for a walk on a Sunday. I can't remember the last play I went to.

I have, however, made new rules about how I will live my life alone as I age. At sixty, a widow for five years, I decided I would no longer seek out friends unless they are women I really want to spend thoughts and time with, and that cut down my list to almost no one. I would not color or perm my hair but would keep it neat and uncomplicated, a cut that only needed a brush and two ears.

I would not participate in fads of any sort: popular movies, books, vacation spots, i phones, TV shows, especially those whose characters are twenty-two and do ridiculous twenty-two-ish things like naked sex and mind-altering drugs. A glass of wine served to alter as much consciousness as I needed to alter. I had early on, after a bad scene at the pipe company, decided I would not work for or with misogynous bosses ever again, a good decision because at fifty-five, the age at which I quit and made this rule, I probably would not have been hired by any kind of boss.

And now, as I push the button on the garage door opener, I understand yet one more time that until a knock sounded at my door, I had been very comfortable with this simple, ruled life.

5

GERALD

Gerald held on to his pack's straps as he stepped into the kitchen. He wasn't sure what would happen next because Alicia had been so quiet on the drive to the house, but he hoped he'd get lunch before he was taken to the next place. It helped, he had discovered, to arrive at the unknown with something in his stomach. When Alicia opened the fridge, lunch looked like a possibility and he set the pack on a chair.

"No." Alicia shook her head. "Not there. In the small bedroom. You look like something the cat dragged in. Go lie down. I'll bring you a sandwich and then we'll decide what to do with you."

Gerald hoped for peanut butter and jam, but he didn't expect the fried egg and mayonnaise sandwich Alicia brought to the bed a few minutes later. His favorite sandwich. "How did you know?" he asked, licking a stream of yolk off the corner of his mouth. "My mom. . ."

"I used to love fried egg sandwiches when I was your age. Maybe most kids do." Alicia sat on the edge of the bed and sipped at a cup of tea. "As you know, I didn't have any children, but I still fry an egg occasionally. Tea? Oh, I forgot. Coffee?"

"No, thank you. It's good just being here making a mess." Gerald wiped at his mouth again.

The room was quiet, except for the sipping and chewing sounds. Then Alicia's cup wobbled dangerously as she leaned toward him. "Tell me again why you believe you are my impossible grandson."

Gerald swallowed, wished he had some water or something to help him say the words he needed. Alicia's body pressing against his legs made it hard to think. Now that he had met the grandma he believed would save him, he knew that this woman wasn't the grandma he had dreamed of. Too skinny, tight lips, suspicious eyes, straight white hair. She was nice, though, sometimes. "I'll try to explain, but it's kind of a long story."

"Go on."

"My mother never told me everything, only that she was born to an Alice Drummond and was adopted by the Graysons a few years after Alice disappeared, having left the baby named Gretchen behind with her parents, who were too old to raise a young child. They gave the little girl to friends, the Graysons who called her Jessie. My mother showed me a picture of herself and the Graysons with Santa at a Christmas party. They looked happy." Even his mother had looked happy, smiling over a shoulder, into a white beard. "Ted and Katherine Grayson."

"I don't know those names. Where did all this happen?"

"In southern Oregon; maybe in California. I remember being little, running around chasing a calf one summer. On a farm."

"Mom told me last year that she had papers that would prove you are my grandmother. But I couldn't understand how that could be. I knew who my grandparents were. The picture showed them."

"Did she ever tell you about your father's family? Maybe those grandparents are who she was thinking about."

"She never did meet them. My father was a construction worker; he lost his job and went to look for another. He promised he'd come back but he never did. All I know about him is that his name was Gerald. Like me."

Gerald was glad when Alicia got up to heat water for tea. And coffee. She called from the kitchen, "And the Graysons? Jessie's adoptive parents? Your adoptive grandfather, mother? Where are they? Do they know you exist?"

"I don't think they are still alive. They didn't come up when I looked for them on the Internet. I remember him when I was little, and he seemed old even then. He ate milk toast for lunch. With canned pears on top." The memory had slipped in like a whisper. Gerald had no idea when the milk toast happened. He was probably about three. Jessie was still Mom. "My mother lost touch with that family. She never talked about them." Gerald didn't want to talk about any of this anymore either, probably like the way his mother felt when he used to ask her questions. "It doesn't matter," Jessie had said more than once. "We have each other. We'll be okay." And Gerald had believed her.

"That's all I know. Then a while ago my mother told me that you were my grandmother, her real mother. She had proof. She had your name written down in her diary."

The kettle whistled and Alicia brought the tea bags and the Bodum pot back to the bedroom. "And how did you find me?" she asked.

"The same way I tried to find everyone else. I Googled you. At the library. You were the only one with your name on Google. You aren't very famous but you were there, something official for a pipe company?" Gerald wondered if he should have said that. He didn't know how to talk to an adult who listened.

The old woman with white hair and the red-headed teenager looked at each other over their cups and it seemed to Gerald that Alicia might be smiling. But all Alicia said was, "A cup of tea is one of life's pleasures."

Gerald could think of other pleasures, a pepperoni pizza, a pair of shoes that fit, a friend's laugh, milk toast. He'd settle for another cup of coffee and a few hours of sleep. He was very tired.

The ringing of a phone somewhere nearby jarred Gerald out of a restless dream that left him breathing in jerks and relieved to be awake. The phone rang six times and he guessed that Alicia must not be home. He pulled himself up, swung his feet to the floor and made his way into the hall. The call must be important, ringing so long. He followed the sound that led him into a bedroom, Alicia's he guessed, the phone next to the bed. "Hello?"

"Well, finally. How's it hanging, Moon?"

Jake. How did he find him? Gerald hung up and dropped to his knees and tried to think what he should do. The phone rang again.

"Leave me alone. I mean it."

"Bet you don't remember telling me your grandma's name, do you?"

"I'm hanging up, Jake. Don't ever call again."

"I'm guessing you've got a sweet deal going there, grandson. Walked by the house a few days ago but it looked like no one was home. Would have gone around back, but a neighbor was staring at me from her front porch so I decided to wait until I was sure you were there. And you are. I'll be there in ten minutes and we can talk."

A click and Jake was gone.

When he knocked, Gerald didn't want to open the door.

"Better let me in, Moon, or I'll start yelling and bring out that nosey neighbor again. I bet your grandma won't like a scene in her front yard. I just need a minute or so to talk to you. C'mon, old buddy."

Jake was right. Alicia would hate a commotion. But Gerald couldn't let him in. "Wait a minute" he called and he found a jacket and went out to the sidewalk where Jake stood, his arms folded across his chest, his lips twisted into his usual cocky smirk below a new fuzz of dark hair.

"That's better." He nodded towards the tall trees at the end of the street. "We can talk down there."

Gerald followed him. When Jake crossed his arms like that, it was like he was holding something in, and Gerald knew that the something was usually anger. He didn't say anything, ready to run if he needed to. But Jake surprised him.

"I really missed you," he said, once they were around the corner. He stopped and he touched the faint smudge of blue still lingered on Gerald's face. "I'm sorry. I don't know what made me do that. I'm glad I found you." He leaned closer to him, but Gerald turned away.

"Don't, Jake. I won't do this anymore. I have been sick, really sick, and I got help from Alicia, even though she says she's not my grandma. She stayed by me in the hospital and we're trying to decide what to do next. She's strict but. . ."

"And she's rich, right?" Jake's hand dropped to Gerald's chin, held him captive. "That's what you're after, isn't it? The money? You think you've got a chance to make the old lady give you a home, clothes, money if you kiss her ass? Play nice?" He tightened his grasp of Gerald's face, "Isn't that it?"

Gerald tried to open his mouth but could only nod.

"Well, I want in on this bonanza, Moon. You owe me. I rescued you, a lost stupid jerk, protected you, taught you how to make it on the street. I didn't have help when I ran away, only hate for a pervert of a stepdad. What I learned from him came in handy for us both. Maybe I should thank him, like you should thank me." Jake snorted, swallowed whatever would have come next. "Fuck it." His fingers tightened on Gerald's chin. "What would grandma say if she knew you had prostituted yourself to pay for the jacket you have on and more important, for the cocaine you love so much? You'd be back to waving that ass on a street corner. And I bet you miss the action."

Jake smelled of pot and dirty underwear as usual; Jake's hair, short as it was, was twisted into greasy spikes; a soul patch completed his do-over. Despite his attempt to change his looks, he was still Jake, a pimp and dealer. That thought unearthed buried memories which sent shards of pain through Gerald's body, scenes of the johns in nice cars unzipping to receive him, the nights Jake waited at his camp for him to come back from the street, his hand out for the cash, the days Gerald did not leave his cardboard bed, so stoned he couldn't get up to pee.

No, Alicia could not know about any of this.

"I'm not doing that stuff anymore. You know that. I quit. The drugs, everything. I want to go to school. I want to meet good people who care about me. I want to care about them, too. I want to live a normal life. "

"I want, I want, I want. That's the trouble with you, Moon. You think you're something special, deserve more than anyone else. Well, you're not, and if you don't believe it, just wait until I tell Mrs. Drummond all about you and see how special you are." Jake's words lifted into the still air, and somewhere in a near yard, a dog barked. "See, that dog agrees with me." His chuckle held a threat.

"What do I have to do?"

"I want you to get in real good with the old lady. Look through the house and her stuff. Find out where she keeps things: money, jewelry, other valuable stuff like stamps, coins, and get her to explain the alarm system to you."

"How can I do that? She doesn't seem to trust me very much and she's trying to find a different place for me to go." Gerald blinked away the sting in his eyes. Jake didn't frighten him. But Jake's plan was killing a dream he hadn't had a chance to dream. And the idea of a grandmother he almost knew.

"Just play your sweet blue-eyed, red-headed innocent self. Convince her you need her. Get sick again. Or even better, convince her she needs you. If you do this good enough, she might not even suspect you being in on it." He winked as if this was the best part of his plan.

Gerald hated to be called sweet. Fifteen-year-old guys should be tough, not sweet. His mother had called him, "sweet." Sometimes the men whose cars he'd climbed into called him that too. Even when he talked tough, said fuck and shit and cunt, he knew he still came off as freakishly...sweet. He wasn't sure why and he didn't know what to do about it.

Right now, he couldn't think about it. Jake waited. The idea was impossible. Alicia would suspect, wouldn't she, if her home was robbed a few weeks after he had moved in? It made his stomach twist to even think of agreeing to what Jake is asking.

"You'll get a cut, you know. We can make this happen while the two of you are together, maybe on a little trip somewhere for a few days."

The dog barked again.

"I have to go back. She'll be home soon."

"Go for a walk in two days, late in the afternoon. I'll meet you at the park down the street, at the bench by the roses. I wouldn't think about not cooperating, Moon. Nothing good would come of that decision." His grip would leave another bruise.

6

ALICIA

The garden has gotten away from me in the past few days. Gerald is sleeping and I have time to myself. I pull on my gloves and when my knee objects, I lower myself onto my buttocks and begin working on the patch by the patio. I've always liked the quiet, thoughtful action of pulling weeds and the green smell of perennials pushing up out of spring-moist soil, a time to let one's mind wander everywhere. Right now, mine is thinking about being famous on Google, but I'm not very, Gerald had said. Actually, Fred had been famous in a local sort of way. He would have been easier to find than me, if they had whatever Google is thirty years ago.

I'm about to move to another weedy bed when Gerald comes out to the patio with our usual drinks. I join him at the table, glad for my tea. He looks tired, dark shadows under his eyes. Can I send this sick, damaged boy out onto the streets again, even if he is lying?

"Your mother had proof?" I still need to learn more.

Gerald hesitates. "My mom had lots of proof about lots of things. She kept receipts and notices and old checks and pictures of her bruises and eviction notices, bills she hadn't paid, anything with her name on it, in a big plastic bag. She'd go through her papers over and over again trying to find proof that she hadn't done something or had done it or didn't owe someone or that someone owed her.

"Bruises?"

"Once she threatened to take Louie to court when he grabbed her arm and she said she had to go to the ER. The photos she had were from one of those photo booths that you go in for a dollar and click on yourself, and they would prove her injuries, she said. But she couldn't find the hospital bill. I guess that there wasn't one. A few days later, Louie, who didn't stick around much longer, told me that she had been stepping into traffic on a narrow bridge when he grabbed her arm and pulled her back onto the sidewalk. She kept those pictures for a long time, hoping, I guess, he would show up again."

The boy's mother is a drunk, I decide. And maybe psychotic, collecting that meaningless stuff and carrying it around. I pick up the tray and tell Gerald I'm going to take a nap. We'll talk later.

Meaningless stuff and carrying it around.

An appropriate description of quite a few people, including myself.

A storm of thoughts will not let me sleep. Turn them off, I tell myself. Breathe deeply, pay attention to the air moving in and out of my body, tell myself "cool in" and "warm out" to disperse the knots of words bumping about like horses in a corral. The mantra works for about three minutes, and then the words stampede in again, a swirl of memories. Mother. I've never been a mother, no regrets, at least now. Perhaps my mother didn't want a child either. Helen, the name I always called her, Helen wanted to be known as a doctor not a housekeeper/child bearer. Helen set a perfect table, read the right books, talked in a warm controlling voice, not only to her patients but also to her child and husband. I can still hear her. "You may be right, but the latest article in *The Wall Street Journal* says. . ." Helen never lost an argument. Especially those she had with me.

I turn over, groan. I have my mother's genes, both in attitude and in arthritis. I move my hip and adjust my knee and the ache lessens. I never have been able, though, to rid myself of her genetic self-righteousness, even when Fred occasionally let me know he was tired of me always being so assured about everything. "God, Alicia, give me a break. I can manage my own life without your constant..." He probably would have said "bitching" if I hadn't turned away from him, sending him into the place we didn't talk about, and then back to the newspaper.

I nagged him about seeing a doctor when he complained of chest pains. Maybe the nagging was why he didn't make an appointment. Just as I had ignored my mother's warnings before my wedding, and then years later, I, in a weak moment, confessed the loss of a lover, of a child, heard her say, "You married badly. I told you so." I didn't say "I told you so" to Fred when his heart attack killed him.

Guess I'm learning to nag too, Fred whispers.

I know I'll not get any sleep. The tea is keeping me awake and anxious. I sit up and try to think of what to do about the boy in my guest room. I don't have an answer, maybe because I'd never had a child to worry about. I need advice and I can't ask Google. I look at the phone at my bedside. Though I don't like her much, this time Betsy, not Google Agnes, will perhaps have some ideas, with her brood of four daughters and who knows how many grandchildren now. I wish I had been more sympathetic years ago when Betsy spent entire coffee hours after church venting about one daughter or another. Perhaps Betsy hadn't noticed my disinterest.

I find the telephone number in my old black book and dial. My fingers are shaking for some reason. Age or anxiety? Age, most likely. I'm not that anxious, am I?

"Hello, Alicia. What a surprise!"

I still cannot get used to the idea that phones know one's name. "Betsy, I haven't seen you for ages. Do you have time for a cup of coffee? I'd love to know how you're doing." Why do I say that? I should just come out with it, tell the woman the real reason I am calling. "Or are you too busy with your grandchildren and all?" How can I climb out of this pit of niceness?

Betsy laughs. "I'd love to see you, Alicia. I'm here alone for once

and have a little carrot cake to share with you. Come right now before Jeffie comes in from school and finishes it off."

I leave Gerald asleep and walk the five blocks to Betsy's house. I
sense herbal tea when the door opens. Betsy hugs me and her soft
neck smells of strawberries. She's rounded out, has smooth cheeks
and a well-cut cap of new auburn hair. "It's been way too long," she
says. I endure the hug, and allow myself to be led into the kitchen
where a cake waits at the table. As Betsy pours from a teapot, she
asks, "Something has happened?"

"Yes."

Our drinks have cooled and only a small piece of cake is left for
Jeffie, who turns out to be a neighbor's boy whom Betsy watches
each day for an hour or so until his mother comes home from work.
"Everyone is busy, working, in school, or moved away—all four of
my girls. I needed a little kid to remind me of the joys of parent-
hood." Betsy glances at me and says, "Oh," and stops. "You wanted
to talk, not listen to me. . ."

"That's why I'm here. I have a grandchild problem, except he's
not my grandchild, and I don't know what to do with him. I thought
you might have some ideas."

I tell Betsy about finding Gerald on my doorstep and his claim
to be my grandson, and then his shocking illness, and my reluctance to send him out into the street again. "Is there any safe
place he can go?" I ask. "Maybe you know a family who would
take him in?"

Betsy frowns. "Most folks hesitate to take in a kid who's left
home. For some reason, they don't feel the same about rescue
dogs. Life on the streets is frightening to imagine. Damages some
kids." Her fingers pat down a straying strand of hair on her forehead and she says, "New haircut, color unknown to anyone on this
earth. Not sure it's me." She laughs and I'm glad I don't have to
comment. "Sorry, I'm still getting used to this younger me. Not sure
it's working."

"Why not? At our age, we can do whatever we want." Do I really
believe that?

"I think so too." She gets back on track. "From what I've heard from the high schoolers in the neighborhood, street kids haven't many safe places to go. The agencies that deal with them don't have the money to house all of them and, of course, some kids don't want to be put into the places that have room for them. They get used to the lifestyle of the camps and ..."

"Gerald was being beaten up in one of those camps."

"Drugs?"

"I suppose. And sex, yes. He is getting over a bout of syphilis that made its presence known last week.

"And you are sure he's not your grandchild?

"Remember I have no children, Betsy."

Betsy pauses, says, "You've gotten to know him a little. Have you thought about asking him to stay with you? You have room, I'm guessing."

I push my chair back and stand up. "Of course not. I haven't had anyone else in around since Fred died twenty years ago. Just a few days have been unnerving." I reach for my purse. Betsy is a perfect grandma with perfect grandchildren. No STD's here. And no help for a non-grandmother of a street kid. "Thank you. I don't know why I thought you could help me."

As I open the door, Betsy slips behind me and touches my shoulder. "I have an idea. My granddaughter Regan is staying with me, taking classes in summer school, while her parents are in Europe. She's pissed that they aren't taking her with them and I bet she'd like some company. Bring your boy by, Gerald, isn't it? some afternoon. I'll get a good movie or something. They won't have to talk much, just eat Cheetos."

I am stunned. Out of the blue, a not-quite-friend offers Cheetos and perhaps an afternoon that might ease some of the anxiety in me and the loneliness I'm beginning to sense in Gerald, especially now that I'm choosing what we watch on TV.

"I'm quite good with teenagers, Alicia. If you decide to ask him to stay, I'll be glad to spell you once in a while. And the kids might like to have a little relief from old ladies." No hug this time. "Call me. I also have a pile of books on raising difficult children for me to review and then lend to you."

Fred would have welcomed Gerald into our home. He liked young people, even volunteered for a couple of years as a tutor in a nearby high school. He invited Raoul, a Spanish-speaking six-teen-year-old to dinner once, to celebrate the boy's passing grade in English lit or maybe it was history, and when I fussed about what I would feed a child growing up on tortillas, Fred brought home a bucket of chicken. The two males ate with greasy fingers, grinning at each other. I made myself a salad and told Fred never to do that again. And he didn't, taking Raoul and others I am sure, to restaurants that teenagers like the ones he worked with felt comfortable in: McDonalds, Taco Bell, other fast food places that surrounded the high school, places that made me shudder when I passed by them.

Gerald would probably like those places, too. If they served food without eyes. I arrive at my door obsessing about a kid I know nothing about, that I do not trust, who is disrupting my life in a way that is frightening me--I cannot keep doing this. And I find him sitting on the front steps. "Sorry," he says. "I went for a walk and locked myself out. Not used to thinking about keys." He stands up. "And I'm a little hungry now. I'm thinking about milk toast."

I open the front door, let Gerald go in first so he will not see my pursed lips. *I will make you milk toast, whatever that is,* I think, *but I will not get an extra set of keys if that's what you are hinting at. You won't be here that long.*

A bit harsh, Fred whispers. Whose side is he on, anyway?

However, I do have to go to the grocery store. I've run out of asparagus and food without eyes. I leave Gerald pining for milk toast but biting into an apple. Shopping is once–a–week excursion in my car because my most inexpensive grocery store is three miles away, the rough road not amenable to an old lady pushing a wire cart. More than once I've nearly ended up head first in the middle of a street, one wheel of my cart caught in the streetcar tracks. The parking at Safeway is not safe either, but if I go slow and watch what is happening on the right side of my car, I can usually pull into the parking spot without a problem. I'm glad that the sedan next to me shows signs of old lady misjudgments too. Her crushed front fender cheers me up.

When did I ever get so timid? Every red stop sign makes my heart beat a bit faster; every yellow light throws my foot on the brake. I used to drive a little MG/TD. No gas gauge, shift up and down, double clutching, cloth windows flapping. That was, of course, after Fred died and I spent a year or two unleashed. I learned to swear a little then, but now I mostly do it in my head. No one wants to see a white-haired old lady lose control.

So here I am, safely parked at Safeway, a list in hand. I always take a list because I get distracted by the millions of possibilities as I go up and down the aisles. I am shopping for a person who doesn't eat food with faces, who craves coffee in the morning, who should use a different shampoo than mine for his curly hair. I also will pick up a few bottles of Sauvignon Blanc, for me.

My cart is filled to the top by the time I get to the cash register. Milk, ice cream, hamburger buns, meatless patties, frozen French fries, apples, banana, Cheerios, a five-dollar loaf healthy bread, eggs, and of course, asparagus and tomatoes. And a couple of frozen dinners for me if this food frenzy ends with me discovering I still don't like to cook.

"They also love Cheetos." Betsy stands beside me, glancing at my basket. She pokes at my groceries. "Good choices but where is the peanut butter?"

"I don't know what to do with him."

"He must have family somewhere. Don't suppose he wants to return to a place he ran away from. Does he have any friends?"

"None. At least none that he talks about."

"Maybe we can kill two worries with one stone. I'll suggest a Coke date with Regan. Who knows? They might be good for each other."

When I get home, into the garage with no new nicks, I'm feeling good. I'm not sure why. I still have the same problem, a teenager making claims on me, but I have tofu and asparagus to offer him. When I find him, he is lying on his bed hugging a pillow, and he looks at me with dim eyes.

"What?" I ask

"Nothing. Just something I have to think through."

I also had things to think through when I was younger. Most of the time I wanted to do it alone. "Okay. Let me know when you are ready for tofu burgers. In fact, let me know when you are ready to cook them. I'm a little leery of meat without eyes."

The music, if that is what it is, blasts into the living room the next morning. I close my newspaper and wish I were comfortable asking Gerald to turn down his clock radio to a reasonable low rumble. But it is obvious that Gerald is lonely, unhappy, and except for an old lady who can't enter his world, not even his music world, he has no one to talk to. Asking him to turn it off seems cruel, like denying him the Cheerios I have just set out on the table. "Breakfast, Gerald," I call over the thumps beating on my eardrums.

"Too loud? You should have told me."

We eat without talking and I, watching him crunch through his bowl of cereal, decide to take up Betsy up on her offer. It can't hurt, can it? It will get Gerald away from this house, maybe find someone who speaks his own language. "A friend has invited you to come meet her granddaughter who is about your age and is lonely because the rest of her family is traveling in Europe. Do you want to go?"

Gerald looks up. "I guess."

A phone call to Betsy sends us walking past the park and up to the door where Betsy stands, waving. I detect a confused look of relief and doubt on the woman's pleasant face and I am feeling the same way. The teenagers examine each other without smiling, exchange hi's when we introduce them, Gerald and Regan, and at Betsy's direction they take Cokes out to the patio and sit down at the picnic table.

Betsy watches them and whispers, "Well, we'll see . . .At least she's not in hiding her room glued to her smart phone. We haven't said a word to each other in hours." Both kids, one blonde, one coppery, are good-looking, each in her or his own way. A long flow of hair swoops across Regan's eyes, followed by a flip of a hand. Gerald draws fingers through his curls, pulling one straight then letting it recoil. They both raise their cans of soda to their lips. Then Gerald says something and Regan gives him a slow grin.

"Thank God. She's going to talk." Betsy pours tea and we move to the living room. "She's so angry and I don't really blame her. Her parents have let her get away with things for years, including a worrisome social life. Then the school cracked down, is making her go to summer school. My daughter and her husband are very involved in their business, are making a lot of money, have always had a nanny when the kids were small, treated their children like addendums to their lives. Cooper discovered early on that he could blame Regan for everything that went wrong during the day. He learned to be innocent and sweet and got his way every time. Regan learned to be angry with everyone and she got her way. The nannies came and went."

"And now they've left her with you?"

"We used to get along pretty well. She seemed to like the fact that she understood the rules here in my house, and she liked me because I paid attention to her, especially when she was smiling. But then her private school called, reported on her cutting classes and told her parents she could not return in the Fall without earning at least one credit in summer school. Meg and Doug shipped her off to me and left for southern France."

"The good brother. . .?"

"He's with them, being good somewhere in the Dordogne," she said, as her eyes in widened in faux astonishment over her coffee cup.

"You don't like him much."

"No. And I am trying to continue to like Regan despite her negative attitude towards me, school and an unfortunate scrape she's gotten herself into. But she is going to classes. At least I think so. I drove her to the school today and picked her up this noon. She has a book or two in her backpack that I've not seen her take out." Betsy's smile wavers and she adds, "I thought if she had a friend. . ."

"Me, too."

The screen door opens and the two teenagers don't look at us as they go into a room I'm guessing is Regan's. The door closes. We do not hear them talking.

"Gaming."

"Like Scrabble?"

"No, like World War Three. Or maybe dystopian chaos. She showed me one day when I insisted, thinking she might be looking at something X-rated. She laughed at me and clicked onto people oozing blood and blowing up cities. I decided it should be X-rated for old people like me. Besides, I am handicapped with arthritis in my thumbs. I'll stick to solitaire."

"Maybe we oldsters need to stick together, sore thumbs and all."

Betsy nods and pours us another cup of tea. She pauses, then adds, "He's handsome, a quiet voice. Shy, I think. Not like the few boys Regan has brought to this house once or twice. Seems like he's trying to work something out. Maybe he's gay? Regan's had a few problems dealing with her own sexual life. Perhaps they'll talk to each other even if they won't talk to their grandmothers." Betsy takes a bag out of a cupboard. "And for you, I have an extra bag of Cheetos. You might need it."

I accept the Cheetos and I understand why she has come to this conclusion about Gerald. I realize, reluctantly, that I have wondered, too. I'm sure, however, that I do not want to return to the pain and uncertainty and lies, yes, the lies that were woven into the fabric of my days with Fred. Why would it be any different trying to live with a gay almost-grandson?

I thank Betsy for her honest words as our teenagers walk into the kitchen apparently finished with World War Three.

Gerald is quiet as we walk home. "Regan asked me to go to a movie with her Friday," he finally says. "Mad Max."

Here we go. I decide to encourage the Regan plan. It's the only plan that makes sense, it's the only plan, period, thanks to Betsy. "Good! Sounds like one I'd probably avoid. You said yes, didn't you?"

Gerald frowns.

"You need some spending money if you're going to movie. Most kids have allowances for stuff like that. We can work it out."

"You shouldn't give me money. You've done so much for me already."

"Oh," I say, remembering Betsy's warning about privileged grandkids. "You will earn your allowance by. . ." I think. Not cleaning toilets. No one wants to do that, even when they are one's own toilets. Not doing the wash. He probably would ruin things, not having a washing machine in his life lately . . . "By clearing the dishwasher every evening." That sounds appropriate. Who am I to know? I've never had a teenager before.

Gay or not.

"Yeah, that's good. And I can vacuum when the house needs it. I'll call Regan when we get home and tell her okay."

Today feels like it might be a good day.

7

GERALD

After hearing Jake's plan, Gerald knew what he had to do. He had to disappear. May be not go to Mad Max on Friday. Not even be around on Friday.

"Burger time," he heard Alicia call. "Not sure what these burgers are made of, but definitely not things with eyes. Maybe not even vegetable, from the looks of them. It's up to you, Gerald, to do something with these frozen pucks."

Gerald blinked, cleared his head. "I'm coming."

The pucks tasted okay with tomatoes and mustard. Even Alicia thought so. "Different strokes for different folks," she said as she took another bite and chewed. Gerald took that as a sign of approval.

"What's on the TV tonight?"

"Only crap," Alicia answered. Gerald had noticed that Alicia seemed to have broadened her vocabulary lately. Maybe she's thinking she is speaking young people's language.

"Mostly shit," he corrected. "But a good old movie is on. *Harold And Maude*, you know, about a kid and an old woman who get it on."

"Science fiction, right? I hate science fiction."

"They call it paranormal now, I think."

"Definitely not of this world. But maybe imaginable. It's good?"

This is what Gerald was hoping, that Alicia would get caught up in a movie and not notice the missing car keys, the empty guest room, the full bowl of Cheetos when she wakes up at the end of the movie.

"Yep. It's really good. You'll like it. I'll get you a glass of wine and we'll chill out with Harold and Maude."

The movie had been running for one hour and ten minutes and Alicia was still sitting upright the maroon armchair, its faded cushion dented from years of evening TV, the half-empty bottle of wine on the end table next to her. "Best fun in a long time," she said, crunching Cheetos, licking her fingers.

Gerald needed time to pack, find the keys, drive somewhere away from Alicia and Jake. Anywhere. He hadn't taken Drivers' Ed in any of his high schools, but he had been in enough slow-moving cars with time to observe how they started, stopped. Maybe just to the train station. Or maybe the bus station, a few blocks from the overpass?

"If you're thirsty, I bought some bottled water. Help yourself." Alicia's eyes never left the screen.

Gerald slid off the sofa and went to his bedroom and began to pack his stuff. He was wrapping a pair of underpants around the book he had carried since the day he had taken it from his mother's bed stand, when the door opened.

Alicia looked at the clothes stacked on the bed as she stepped into the room, but she did not come closer. "You can't run away, Gerald. Whatever it is will just follow you wherever you go."

Had Alicia had been reading his mind? He had to tell at least part of the truth. "I have to leave, Alicia, before both of us get hurt."

Still motionless, she continued, "I saw a missed call recorded on the phone. I called the number. An incoherent person mumbled at me. One of your friends, I imagine. He called again today. Same number. He didn't answer when I dialed back. I think you're in trouble, Gerald. You can't run away again." Alicia held orange-tinged fingers out toward him, seemed to be trying to take his hand. "We can stick together, like Harold and Maude. We can, can't we?"

Her grandmother was wobbling, possibly drunk. Gerald took her hand and led the old woman to her bed. "Sometimes the TV can be like our Bible. . ." Alicia philosophized as Gerald pulled the quilt over her. . . "and teach us lessons."

"For sure, Alicia. See you in the morning." Gerald couldn't remember ever being offered a Cheetos-yellow hand, or any kind of hand like this one, warm, tinged with the color of love, maybe.

He brought Alicia her breakfast in bed the next morning.

"I haven't been intoxicated for years." Alicia shook her white hair off her forehead, not apologizing, maybe even bragging. "You're loosening me up a little, I think."

"No, the wine loosened you up, Alicia. I pushed you into drinking it, with all those Cheetos."

"The only embarrassing part was the way I felt compelled to lick my fingers after each mouthful. Sorry if I was. . ."

Gerald supplied the word Alicia was looking for. "Gross. But that's what you are supposed to do with Cheetos."

"Live and learn. But I was worried, am worried. About you. We need to talk."

Gerald had spent part of the night trying to come up with a story about Jake that would make sense to his grandmother. A former friend, Gerald would say, who claimed Gerald owed him something, a concert ticket. Harmless, but his friend was nuts. He would tell Alicia that he had decided to escape this guy by packing and leaving. But then he remembered her words from evening before. "But you're right, Alicia. I can't run away. I need to face up to Jake, tell him to leave me alone, threaten to call the police, or something. I'll meet him one more time, in the park down the street, and let him know he has to stop bothering me".

Alicia listened, her lips straight and unsmiling. "He's not a danger to you?"

Gerald shook his head, said no. He breathed a little easier. The story might have bought him some time to decide what to really do about Jake. And to decide what to do about Alicia. The one thing he **had** figured out is that running away wasn't an option. Not right then, at least.

When Gerald went to the porch to pick up the newspaper and he saw Jake, pushing off from the step he'd been sitting on, and he realized he had run out of time.

"Hi, Moon," Jake sneered and reached out and touched his arm.

"Gerald, you should come in."

"No, it's all right, Alicia. We'll stay right here. I have to tell him something."

Alicia left the door ajar when she went back into the house, as if she thought Gerald might need an escape route. But all Gerald was going to do was tell Jake that he'd thought it all over, that he wouldn't do what Jake wanted him to do.

But Jake's fingers squeezed on his arm, like usual.

"I waited in the park yesterday afternoon," he whispered. "You didn't come. One more chance, Moon. Tomorrow morning. Alone. The park. 9:30. Be there or your pleasant little life will be all fucked up. I've found a witness or two who will swear to your activities under the overpass and in a lot of cars."

"Who will believe your doped-up friends? Most of the time they can hardly keep their eyes open, much less remember anything that happened weeks ago." Then Gerald remembered Dougster.

Dougster dealt all kinds of drugs. He also dealt with the cars that slowed down as they passed under the overpass, their drivers looking, some smiling, some squinting, at the kids standing on the sidewalk. When they nodded, a girl or a boy would walk out, open the car door and be driven away for a while. When they returned, they pulled crumpled bills out of pants pockets, handed them to Dougster, his reward for being their protector, he told them. He handed out wet wipes and condoms as part of his services. Jake became a partner in the business when Dougster expanded his activities to another street on the east side, and soon Gerald, Jake watching, had been nodded at and taken away.

The first time it seemed okay. Gerald was high, pot smoke still in his lungs, when he climbed into the car. The john was soft-voiced, only asked him to take him in his mouth, thanked him as he gave him three fives and dropped him off a few blocks away. "Keep one of those for yourself," he advised. "You did good."

But Jake had pulled a knife out of his jacket pocket when he found the extra bill hidden under Gerald's belt. "You get what I give you. Or this. Remember that next time." And there were the next times, after Jake began offering him cocaine and Gerald discovered he liked it. A lot.

Of course, Dougster would be in on Jake's plan to rob Alicia. Not only would his stories force him to cooperate, but he'd help Jake get away with the haul. Dougster had a truck.

"9:30 tomorrow. I'm doing something in the afternoon and Alicia will suspect something is wrong if I don't show up. So, leave." He shouted the last two words, in case Alicia was listening in the hallway.

He needn't have worried. Alicia was curled up on the flowered patio chair, turning the pages of a book. She looked up at Gerald and said, "That, I hope, is the last of him." She didn't wait for an answer. "Don't forget to call Regan about the movie tomorrow. I told Betsy that I can pick you up afterwards if you need a ride home." Gerald saw that when Alicia smiled, she looked different – more like a grandmother.

Gerald couldn't sleep thinking about Jake and his fingers on his arm, his grip on his life.

"Going for a walk," he called the next morning after he'd emptied the dishwasher. He threw on his jacket and headed for the park. Jake was waiting on a bench, huddled against the soft mist that hung on the trees, his hoody pulled over his head, his narrow eyes watching.

"You're alone," he said. He was his usual suspicious self.

"Who else would I have brought? A cop? I don't want anyone else to know about this plan of yours any more than you do. So, talk."

Jake lit a cigarette, exhaled in his fake-casual way, said, "Two weeks from today. You get the old lady out of the house and we go in. You have two weeks to search the place, make a list of the stuff we will want: electronics, jewelry, fur coats, money, art, silver, anything we can sell including drugs, liquor, credit cards, antiques. . ." He paused, apparently out of things to steal and fingers to count them on, high on something, sneaking paranoid glances over his shoulder as he talked.

Gerald had to find a way to stop Jake. "Three weeks. And you will be disappointed with what she has. She doesn't do electronics at all, only a TV, no smartphone, computer of any kind. I haven't seen any fur coats or jewelry and only a few meds. Miralax, Musinex, baby aspirins, old lady stuff, all lined up in her bathroom cabinets." Gerald dismissed the list with a wave of a hand. "Nope, I'm pretty sure she doesn't take painkillers," he added, "except for maybe ibuprofen for her sore knee. I checked her bathroom when I moved in, looking for something for my stomach. I only found a dried-up bottle of Pepto-Bismol and ended up at the hospital, with no drugs to bring home."

"Forget the drugs. Find where she keeps her credit cards, if she has a safe and where she keeps keys to the car, garage. Alcohol. I saw through the window that she's got arty stuff all around that must be worth something. Make a list."

Time. Gerald needed more time. "How can I do that? She's always there."

Jake stood up, adjusted his crotch and groaned. "Get her out of the house," he growled, glancing around before he started walking away in the opposite direction from which Gerald had come. "You'll be sorry if you don't. Two weeks. I'll be back." His twitchy attempt to appear in control would have been laughable, but Gerald had seen him like that before. Meth. Jake didn't answer except to turn and slink away down the path.

8

ALICIA

So, this is how it feels to have a child. One moment a small surge of joy, the next an overwhelming sense of dread. Where is Gerald? He said he was going for a walk but he's never done that before. I don't see him from the front porch and I go back inside and without thinking why, go to the Gerald's room. The door is open an inch, an invitation to open it further, go in, look around. The bed is unmade; clothes are spread over chairs, scattered on the floor. He doesn't have much, and what he does have is out of the backpack and lying about like piles of garbage. Do I have the right to ask my tenant to keep his room picked up? Do I even have the right to be in this room?

No, but something catches my eye. A tattered book tucked under a pillow. I lift a corner of the pillowcase, read the title: *My Diary*. Gerald keeps a diary. I hear footsteps on the porch. I retreat, leave the room, and go to greet him.

"Fine," he answers when I ask how the walk was. He's frowning like he's upset but what do I know of teenagers? He goes into his bedroom and closes the door tightly. Against me.

I've had a door closed against me before. The memory still lingers after years of trying to bury it. I need to sit down in my old chair, try again to bury the memory for good.

I thought he loved me, and he did, I suppose, but not enough to end two marriages. Jason worked at the pipe company. I hired him, in fact, in my role of Human Resources Director, instantly attracted to his crooked teeth, his direct brown-eyed gaze, his long fingers. He also was well qualified for the position he was applying for—I wasn't that easily led off track. But I did go off track later. I invited him, months after he started working in a nearby office, often waving at me through my office window as he passed by, to a TGIF drink. After several of this sort of innocent-seeming meetings, he invited me to his temporary home, an apartment nearby, temporary because his wife and child would be following as soon as the school year was over and they'd be looking for a house.

I accepted the invitation because I had been treading water in a pool of self-doubt for the whole eight years of my marriage, close to drowning in it at times. I'd dog paddled, kept my head above water, turned down occasional propositions from men I met on business trips, but the desperation I felt as I approached Jason's door that first night overcame any sense of danger.

He was an excellent lover. Patient, creative, his gentle fingers talented in orifices of all sorts. I had never been loved like that, and I sometimes I still feel a ripple of pleasure when I think of his hands, hands that taught me that my body could receive and give joy. I had not felt this sort of love with Fred. A part of me that I had only suspected existed awakened, the part of me hidden under the cloak of acceptance that enveloped my marriage. I wanted this awakening to go on forever.

I also wanted to be Fred's friend forever.

And for a while, I believed it could be that way. That Fred would understand when he learned of the man who was experiencing me in a way he could not. That Jason would remain a lover, a part of my life, as pleased as I when he heard the news I had to tell him, good news, I thought. Stupid, naïve, impossible dream, I know now.

My lips trembled against his ear, fingers brushing his cheeks, I whispered, "I'm pregnant."

I felt his body stiffen, his face twitch. "And?" he asked.

"And . . ." And then I understood. "This child yours, I promise." I kissed his hot cheek, one last effort to pull him into my dream.

Jason rolled away from me, sat up. "No. It is not. You are married. The child is your husband's." He looked back over his shoulder at me. "I was careful every time. Remember?"

"Almost every time. And Fred has taken care to not have sex with me at all, for years. You know that. This child is yours, Jason." I tried to touch his neck. He pushed my hand away, stood up.

"My God, Alicia. I will not break up my family over this stupid mistake. It isn't fair to anyone, especially to my wife and child, who have moved in now that the school year is over. She's pregnant with our next child. This romp has been good, you and me, but not so good that I would hurt her."

By then I was sobbing, wiping my nose on the sheet, choking out words in gurgles. "I'm the one who ends up hurt?" But he had walked out the door. As his car roared away, I was left empty of dreams.

I lied when I asked for help from the company's nurse, claiming one of our employees was in trouble. She knew of a doctor who would help. And he did. I transferred Jason to another division of the company, away from my office. I went on with the marriage I had contracted to, hoping that things between Fred and me would change, that he'd learn he could love a woman. He didn't, of course, but I knew he valued me and the passionless, calm life we were creating. I grew accustomed to it.

Over time, I found I could control my flood of self-doubt by becoming a strong-willed, respected businesswoman. And I learned to achieve a sort of physical satisfaction with a series of vibrators that brought explosive orgasms but had no arms to hold me and no man crying oh God in my ear.

Gerald is quiet behind his door. Maybe he needs a smart phone to entertain him, like Betsy's granddaughter? What is a smart phone? I should ask. I reach for my ordinary phone, dial Betsy's number, pretend I'm wondering if I should drive the two to the theatre. As I suspected, Betsy has it all under control but she asks if I'd like to go to an Art Fair on Friday. "The kids can do what they want, in the afternoon, and the grandmas," Betsy says, "can do what they want."

"I need to know what a smart phone is," I answer, and Betsy laughs.

When I mention the plan to Gerald, he grins. "You two can go to an Art Fair, whatever that is. In the afternoon, I'll connect with Regan and we'll go to a movie, have a latte at Starbucks." He seems glad that I'm getting out with someone who might be a friend. I feel the same about him.

I lie down for a bit, but can't nap, a new thought inserting itself into my attempt to restore quiet into at least an hour of my life. I roll over onto my good hip and raise my body, push my legs over the edge of the bed, my feet seeking the slippers I'd placed there. I must do something to help Gerald overcome his abysmal past, the rejection by his mother, sexual experiences I can only guess at. The boy should be in school. He needs to learn he is as good, in fact, better than other kids with whole families because he has courage and a life I that makes him stronger than most of them will ever be. I am convinced of this. Why, I'm not sure, but I can still feel a young firm hand holding my Cheetos fingers.

A good school will be expensive. Perhaps it is time to not only clean out my closets, but to straighten out other assets, including the jewelry I reluctantly inherited from Fred's mother who liked to wear a small fortune on her body. I haven't looked at the old jewelry box for years but I remember where I hid the screwdriver that would get me into Fred's homemade safe. I find the tool in a bathroom drawer and first try kneeling, but my knee complains, so I drop to the floor, sit, legs crossed, in front of it, and unscrew the metal register covering heat duct next to the bed. When we first moved into this house, Fred closed off this duct and installed a metal shelf to hold his passport, birth certificate, extra checkbooks, and other papers he considered valuable in the space behind the register. He had read about this project in a magazine and I remember laughing at the idea.

Now who's laughing, Fred asks, leaning over my shoulder. I thought you had gone, I whisper.

No such luck, Alicia. You still need me.

The old jewelry means nothing to me and I've not thought of the "safe" for years. My own jewelry, such as it is, is under my sox in my dresser.

I use the screwdriver to pry loose the register held captive by at least one thick coat of paint, the paint also begin-again project after I'd buried Fred. It falls to the floor. The jewelry box, dusty, comes out easily and the screwdriver is successful in getting it open. Inside, rings, pearls, and diamond earrings greet me, rustling as I dip my fingers into the container. Some of the silver is gray with tarnish, but most is unaffected by being ignored for twenty or more years. The horde invites me to pick it up. I do, gathering earrings like colorful peanuts in my palm.

How I had disliked my ostentatious mother-in-law. Fred had been her favorite child, a perfect boy, her only child whom she compared often to the inferior offspring of her friends. When he married me, untalented, unmoneyed, her bitter words at the wedding said it all. "Take care of my son," she hissed as I clung to the sleeve of the rented tuxedo pressing against my arm and tried to look unafraid. This was not her last piece of advice. Whenever she and I came together in family scenes, directives soared like missiles at me as I cooked dinners, passed hors d'oeuvres, waved goodbye. The years passed, and I made sure these occasions occurred less and less often. I imagined one time, when her soft, menacing voice accused me of carelessness with Fred's medications, that I would enlighten this sanctimonious woman about the disease her son was secretly suffering from. I didn't. The mother died before the son. Her jewelry went to her inadequate daughter-in-law, even though she probably would rather have preferred to have been buried wearing it.

She's gone. Time to stop thinking ugly thoughts about a dead woman, especially since the small fortune I'm pouring back into the box on the floor in front of me will be going toward a good a cause.

I use the screwdriver one more time and attach the register back on the wall. Using my hands, I push my body into a hump, like a camel, and then pull myself upright. "When did it get so hard to get up off the floor?" I wonder out loud as I place the box on my dresser. Now I am tired enough to go to sleep.

The next morning, I smell frozen waffles toasting as I dress. For a moment, I can't remember what I've scheduled today, but it comes to me as I comb my hair. Art Fair. Betsy. I hear Gerald calling, "Be up and be a' doing, Alicia. You have a date coming by soon."

How good it feels to have someone greet me when I wake up. I decide to wear my black trousers and a cream silk blouse to the Art Fair, my old lady's uniform when my destination was more than the usual grocery store. Earrings? Yes. The box on my dresser will have a pair that will add a little color to my outfit. Small red rubies that swing like cheerful raindrops from my ears are just right. Gerald tells me this when I slice into a waffle minutes later.

"Lookin' good, Alicia," he says. Amazing what dressing up a little can do for one's outlook. I *feel* good. I grab my purse and answer the doorbell.

"See you this afternoon, Gerald." I open the screen door and wave at Betsy.

"Don't hurry back on my account," he answers. "I'll be with Regan most of the afternoon."

In the car, Betsy sighs and tells me that Regan smiled this morning. "Maybe she just needs a friend."

"Yes," I answer.

The Fair is outdoors, tents lined in rows along park paths, eager artists answering questions and watching as we pick up glass vases, ceramic platters, exquisite silver bracelets. I have never seen so many lovely, handmade things. Along the next path, the painters and sculptors show their wares. The two of us stop at times to wonder what the artists are trying to tell us. And sometimes we can't help giggling. "We obviously aren't getting the message here," Betsy says, and I roll my eyes in silent agreement.

I am not going to buy anything. I have too much stuff already. I touch my earrings and think of the other things that have found permanent places in our house, whether I welcomed them or not. The basement is cluttered with boxes of old dishes and books that Fred did not want me to toss, molding under the stairwell.

We wander toward lines of booths. Scents of ginger and saffron make us glance at each other and the nearby food tents. Signs offer tacos and samosas and something called tikis. "Shall we risk street food, Alicia, or are you desiring a real table rather than your lap?

"I'm also desiring a glass of white wine." I have surprised myself and apparently, Betsy.

"Super! I know a quiet little Italian place a few blocks away."

The street quiets as we move away from the bustle of the Fair. "I don't usually drink wine at lunch," hoping she doesn't think I have an addiction of some sort.

"Me either. Except when I'm out to a late lunch with a friend."

"And I don't usually go out for lunch with a friend," I add. "I'm really glad for your invitation." I am about to say thank you, but Betsy takes my arm and directs me into a small restaurant. Dark, smelling of oregano, and even though it is daytime, candles in bottles are lit at each table, the kind of place I used to think of as romantic. A long time ago such environments allowed a certain amount of anonymity, when my meetings demanded secrecy. A world ago. I feel a swoop of melancholy as I sit down.

Betsy sighs. "Despite four kids under fifteen, I was lonely after Mark died. I almost began an affair in this place. Came to my senses at the second glass of Barbera, when I heard him slurp up his spaghetti. That moment of truth saved everything. Amazing how that happens." She pages through the menu. "Do you slurp your spaghetti?" She laughs again. "Never mind. After four kids, I've gotten over that aversion. There are worse things. . ." She looks up at me.

"Yes, there are," I say, but I won't go into my story, not yet. Perhaps on another day, another lunch.

9

GERALD

Thursday, Gerald had volunteered that he could help clean up the silver platters in the buffet and maybe organize some drawers. He wasn't sure how to clean that stuff he'd seen in the dining room, but he needed to be have a reason to be interested in it. He could do the search Friday morning when Alicia was at the Art Fair.

Alicia laughed. "You amaze me Gerald. Your mother must have raised you well, about neatness, at least.

Gerald nodded. "Yeh, when I was little. We had an apartment."

"I'm sorry. None of my business." Alicia smiled as she walked into the hall. Her voice seemed cheerful, not nosey. "I was feeling the same way about your room. Let's have a Spring cleanup only early. My mother used to have the maid roll up the rugs, wax the floors, and she tossed out any clothes that didn't fit anyone anymore." She stood at the door, pointed at the wads of clothing Gerald had thrown around his room.

Gerald shrugged, started picking up his stuff even though Alicia had expanded the cleaning project. His plan would still work. "Okay, today's a cleaning day, Alicia." He hesitated, "Including your own closet which I bet you haven't looked at lately." A few hours working together seemed like an okay idea. Friday morning he'd be alone, able to go through everything else. Gerald was sure he would find nothing of value and he could report to Jake that breaking in would be a lost cause.

"We'll start with your room first. You have fewer things to sort out than I and maybe you'll find that it's easier to put them in a drawer instead of on the floor."

"Haven't had a drawer for a long time." Gerald led the two of them to his bedroom and quickly pulled the blankets up into a smoother lump. "New experience."

As they straightened the pillows, Alicia suggested they wash the bedding. Gerald slipped the diary into his pocket as he removed the pillowcase. Moments later, the sheets were in the washer and Gerald's scattered clothes were headed there, too, including the dingy underwear that no amount of washing would help. Before he could hide it under the rest of the wash, Alicia said, "We'll go shopping for new things tonight."

A couple of hours later, suits, stored in plastic bags and dresses crushed on hangers, made it onto Alicia's bed. "You don't need these?" Gerald saw a flicker of hesitation on Alicia's face as she answered. "These were very good clothes. . . but I have nowhere to wear them anymore. I doubt anyone will want them, so outdated." She lifted a dress up, held it against her body, and Gerald could see what she meant.

The dress was black wool with a white collar. The label at its neckline was made with silver threads. Big shoulders. Probably once a good look for a woman in an office, an important woman in an office, but definitely not one Alicia would wear to the grocery store. "I've heard about consignment stores," Gerald said. That's what his mother had called the Goodwill store where she bought her clothes until one of her boyfriends laughed at her. "Consignment stores sell good used clothes," he had said, "not discarded shit."

"Fuck you," his mother had answered, as she poured herself another drink. Gerald was surprised he remembered that scene. Toward the end of it all. Maybe that was why.

"Good thought. Let's leave these on hangers and plan for a trip in a day or so. Ugly or stained stuff in the bags for Goodwill." Alicia sniffed at the armpit of a jacket and stuffed it into a black bag along with Gerald's old underwear.

Discarded shit.

The closet was nearly empty. A coat, real fur, Gerald guessed, remained in a box, hanging on a hook. Alicia showed him how to fold her sweater and where to put them in the drawers. A black silk suit and a hat still hung on the closet rod. "For funerals," Alicia explained. Sweat suits and tops, slacks and blouses, and a couple of jackets clustered on hangers in one corner of the closet and Alicia moved them to the middle of the closet. They were her good clothes now. She lowered herself to the floor near a pile of shoes. Once she determined that they still fit her, she arranged the shoes under the remaining clothes. "Feet change when you get older. She pointed at a lump on her left foot. "Bad, pointed, too-small shoes. Should have listened to my mother."

That was the second time Alicia had mentioned her mother. "What was she like?"

Gerald had never asked an old person that kind of question— could she remember? Did she, like him, want to forget?

Alicia threw three pairs of shoes towards the Goodwill bag and tried on several others. "My mother, Helen, was a doctor. She detested the term 'household engineer,' popular after the war, as many women returned to their homes from the factories and settled, with some reluctance, into being housewives again. Helen was always a doctor, with lots of advice for me, especially about shoes. And about my choice of men, of a career, about the need for me to be my own person."

Alicia looked at Gerald and pointed at some sandals. "Cute?" At the look on Gerald's face, she tossed them into the bag and continued. "I couldn't understand what she meant until I went to work after a couple of years of college and discovered what it felt like to be in control of one's life, or at least part of it." Alicia turned and looked at Gerald. "Of course, you know what I'm talking about, don't you?"

"I guess." Not about the mother being a household engineer, or about living with other people, but Gerald remembered the day he walked out of the motel room and told himself he was now on his own. "But you didn't hate your mother, did you?"

"Hate? No. Maybe disregard is what I did. I sometimes used the word love when I left for somewhere else, but that was a kind of ritual. I could see she cared, her eyes misted as we said goodbye, but I didn't feel the same as she, only relief. I was free." Alicia raised herself up from the floor and collapsed among the clothes on the bed. She patted an empty spot next to her. "Sit down, Gerald. I haven't thought about any of this in years. I'm feeling very sad at this moment."

Gerald wasn't sure what to say to an old woman trying to smile. Careful not to sit on a loose hanger, he reached out for Alicia's hand and held it.

Alicia murmured, "I don't think I knew what love was until the day Helen died. I chose her burial clothes, watched as she was made as lovely as she had been before the cancer, touched her cold, cosmetic-smooth face, and realized at that moment I had been left with a painfully empty hole inside me, in place where my mother had lived forever. I just didn't know it."

Alicia needed a Kleenex and Gerald let go of her hand and pulled one out of the box on the bedside table. "You had loved your mother without knowing it." He almost wrapped an arm around the slumped shoulder at his side, but Alicia drew away and blew her nose.

"Out of the mouths of babes," she said. "Thank you." She pointed at the clothes on the bed. "How am I going to sleep tonight with all this on my bed?" and Gerald knew that conversation was over.

"There's always the floor, my system." Gerald lifted an armload of dresses and laid them on the rug. The two of them cleared the rest from the bed and decided that they needed to find a consignment store before they could move them again. Maybe they'd find one at the mall after dinner.

Because Alicia still wasn't used to having another person in the house, she had neglected the refrigerator again, which was half empty, especially of vegetables. "Have you ever eaten at Applebee's? There is one close to where we are going, and they have all kinds of food."

"Food without eyes?" Gerald pulled on a sweater. *Does it matter anymore?* "What is nachos?" Alicia asked as the waitress waited.

When Gerald told her, Alicia said, "I'll have a hamburger. They couldn't do anything strange to that, could they?"

"So, no chilies on it?

"God, no. Any other surprises?"

"Blue cheese? Bacon?"

Alicia sighed. "Sure. This is a night for new experiences, it seems."

When they had finished their meal, Gerald began to feel guilty about the stuff they were about to buy and the two of them seemed to have run out of things to talk about. Gerald raised his hand to wave at the waitress to bring them their check when Alicia leaned towards him.

"I was remiss. I was so full of thinking about my own mother, I didn't ask about yours. You've told me a few things about her and you said you hate her. Do you really?"

Gerald sipped on the last of his coffee and had a moment to decide if he would answer. A warm hand on his, a repeat of the afternoon's gesture, encouraged him to say, "Yes, I think so." As he began, Gerald heard his mother's voice under his words. He told how Jessie, at twenty-eight, had a baby, named him Gerald, thought she was set for the rest of her life with a hard-working, red-haired carpenter's assistant working on a nearby construction project. Maybe they were married. Gerald didn't know, but Jessie never took his last name and gave Gerald her own when he was born. For a while, Jessie told him, his father came home every night, they had money to pay the rent, they had a red-haired baby that made them laugh. Then he lost the job because the project was finished and he couldn't find another like it. "At first, my mother said they were brave, were sure they would make it, but that hope slipped away in a mist of pot smoke and then harder drugs. He disappeared."

"Your mother told you this?"

"A long time ago, when she and I found a picture of the three of us, at her grandparents' farm or somewhere, and it made my mother feel bad. I don't remember very much about those days, only what she told me."

Gerald had never put this story into words, only visions of memories. "My mother managed for a year or so on welfare, and we lived for a while with my great grandmother, Sonja, by then a widow and very sick, I don't know of what. She said those months were good ones, despite my grandma's illness. At least we had food, a bed, and a park down the street. Then Sonja died leaving debts that my mother couldn't pay. The farm was lost."

Gerald paused. "I remember wondering how a farm could get lost. Later, everything else was lost. Now the only thing I have of my mother's is a diary. Drugs took over again and I changed schools a lot, making my way back after school to the rooms I called home and finding my mother passed out."

Refilled cups in front of them, Alicia interrupted, "Your mother? She didn't try to quit the drugs? She had a little boy to think about."

"Yeah, she worried about me sometimes, mostly when she was sober and saw what my clothes and I looked like. One time the school counselor followed me to where we were staying, a room in an old house, and my mother promised that things would be better, she had a job, she'd found a Laundromat to do the wash at. 'Do you know how hard it is to keep a kid clean?' she said. I felt like everything was my fault. The counselor backed toward the door and wished us luck. If she reported us to the city's protective agency, I wouldn't know. We moved the next day. I don't remember going to a Laundromat."

Gerald pushed aside his cup. "Mom must have been scared, though, because she disappeared for a few days, then she came back, joined AA again, and for a while we had a normal life, me in school, mom working. I came home to what seemed like a real home. I remember sitting next to Mom, watching TV on the old set that came with the studio apartment we lived in."

"How old were you by then?"

"About eleven. Old enough to notice the difference between me and the other kids, clothes, mothers who waited for their kids

at the end of the day, Christmas. I was never invited to birthday parties and I was sure kids laughed at my homemade Valentines. I got
Valentines because the teacher said if we gave them, we had to give
them to everybody. I kept mine in an old envelope for a long time."
He paused, looked at his hands. "Silly, I guess. Then my mother got
on drugs again and we started moving from motel to motel again.
I was thirteen when I knew for sure that I hated her. I left her sick
and out of it, about a year later, at a motel that offered rooms by
the hour and I'd been kept awake every night by the sounds coming
through the walls. And sometimes from the bed next to mine."

Gerald heard Alicia's soft "Oh God," and knew he couldn't go
on to tell her about what it had been like to live the next three
months on the streets. He couldn't risk it. And he couldn't let Jake
tell it either. No matter what. Alicia, looking into her cup of cold tea,
seemed unable to ask any more questions, which was good. Gerald
took a breath, smiled even though his teeth were dry from talking
so much, and said, "So that's it. I'm ready to go to Target's men's
underwear."

Alicia sat up straight. "You are a brave person." She took her
purse from the back of her chair, got out her credit card, handed it
to the waitress who was holding a pot of coffee. "We're done here,"
she said, as she pulled on her coat.

Friday morning Gerald figured he would have at least three
hours while the grandmas were at the Art Fair to look for whatever
he could report to Jake. Not everything, of course, but enough so
he knew he had tried. The damp basement smelled like old dirty
socks and the boxes fell apart when he opened them. The books
inside were gray with mold. Nothing there, that was for sure.

Upstairs, the only electronics worth anything were the TV and
maybe the portable microwave. Then he found a stack of boxes in
the garage filled with old 78's and a turntable and speakers, probably Fred's equipment. People collected that old stuff, he'd heard.
A chest of forks and knives, and the three or four silver platters
he'd cleaned, plus a stack of dishes wrapped in soft fabric, filled

the buffet. On top of the buffet, Alicia had stuffed a couple of fancy vases with dried flowers, and six shiny candlesticks lined up behind them, the candles still in their cellophane wraps.

He smelled Alicia's powder as he opened the door of his grandmother's bedroom, and for a moment he thought she was in the room. Then he knew it was his guilty conscience making him squirm, and he walked in and around the piles of clothes on the floor to the chest of drawers. A jewelry box he hadn't seen before rested next to a carton of Kleenex on top of the chest. He was careful not to move either as he pushed a finger nail under the box's latch and opened it. A swirl of necklaces and bracelets glowed in the dim light. Earrings, silver and gold, lined up at the edge of the box.

He couldn't resist touching some of the jewelry, the pearl chains, the red and green stones in a gold bracelet and the sparkling flowers and birds covered with stones. He picked up a tangle of gold chain and discovered a grasshopper shimmering with what must be diamonds. A pin, old-fashioned, designed to be worn on a black dress, he guessed. None of this looked like Alicia. Gerald had never seen her wear any jewelry, not even a ring, until today. The box hadn't been in her closet when they went through it, and he hadn't seen anything that looked like a safe. And why was it out in the open, unnoticed when they were in Alicia's room?

He put everything back the way he found it. *I can't let Jake find this treasure*. Gerald tried to think. He couldn't confess he'd been snooping around and warn his grandmother or she'd wonder who might want to steal it. Maybe she'd even suspect Gerald. If he told her about Jake's plan, he would have to tell Alicia about his past and Alicia would never understand why he had gotten into those cars, why he put up with Jake's fists. He didn't understand it himself, really, the cocaine, pills, the giving in, the not caring. Not until he opened the diary and realized how close he had come to becoming just like his mother, felt the kindness of an old man and a tent, the caring hands of an old man with scissors, had he escaped.

Her mother had written a name in pencil on a page of her diary with nothing else on it, a note scribbled in the spur of a moment.

Alice Drummond. In a rare clear moment in the last of the motels, Jessie had held the book open, showed it to Gerald, had torn out the page. "If anything happens to me, this is your grandmother. I saw her name on a birth certificate in some papers." When Gerald asked where the certificate was, her mother shook her head. "Lost it somewhere."

Back in his room, Gerald shook the worn pages of the book one more time, hoping that certificate, the proof, would fall out, but it didn't. Now that he was away from the life under the overpass, from his mother, almost away from Jake, he was beginning to understand how desperate he had been to be loved before Alicia, and perhaps even now.

As Gerald put the book back under his pillow, he tried to think of a time when he felt loved. Maybe, when he was little, not lately. Alicia did care about him, though. Maybe that's almost the same as love. A step on the way to love, maybe. No way could he turn back. He had to tell Jake about the jewelry. Then Jake'd be satisfied, leave him alone, let him learn how to love and be loved. To finally become whoever he really was.

The doorbell startled him into sitting up. He heard Regan calling and when he opened the door, is friend grinned. "I'm a little early, but I have a surprise for you. Let's go down to the park."

Gerald found the key Alicia had given to him as she left that morning and followed his friend out, remembering that the last time he walked this way, it was with Jake. Only Regan's fingers on his sleeve kept him walking.

He was glad she hurried past the bench that he and Jake had sat on and instead led him to a leafy den back in the trees. Empty beer cans made it obvious that others had also discovered this den.

"There's a couple of rocks over there." Regan pointed and Gerald followed her, realizing that his friend had probably squatted at least once at the same rock that she was now lowering her body on to. "Ugh,' Regan groaned. "Wish we could lug a bench back here. We tried but the benches are screwed down."

"What's up?" Gerald asked but he was sure he knew the answer.

"Figured you'd be ready for a smoke after being at the old lady's house for so long. Found this place a few days ago when I met a guy standing near here and he invited me to share a toke with him. I must have looked needy or like I had money because he sold me a dime bag before he left and wanted to know if I would want regular delivery." She tucked a shiny strand of yellow hair behind a hair-clip. "Can you imagine my grandmother's face if a guy in raunchy clothes, the kind of guys you probably knew on the streets, came to our door? Don't look so surprised. Grandma Betsy told me about you being a street kid."

"Did he tell you his name? Leather jacket?"

"God, no. No leather. He really smelled bad, had ratty hair. But his pot was good." Regan pulled a plastic bag from her jacket pocket. "You decide. You had more experience with this stuff than me." She handed Gerald a pipe, the bag, and a lighter.

Gerald couldn't think of a reason to not take the fixings and to pack them into the bowl. He handed the pipe back to Regan. "Host goes first. It's the rule."

When it was his turn to inhale, to feel the first small rush as the smoke entered his lungs, Gerald knew, despite the pleasure of inhaling, he would regret it. The smell, the secretive hidden spot, the rush, brought back other scenes like it but worse: terrible, hurting moments. His stomach heaved. He gave the pipe back to Regan. "It's good," he said, "but I can't do it. I'm on a medicine for a heart thing and I'm going to throw up if I keep..."

"So, it's up to me to finish this?" Regan said, not really asking, inhaling deeply, not looking disappointed at Gerald's turning down her offer. "Next time?"

"Sure." Gerald waited for his almost-friend to finish her smoke wondering how long he would be haunted by those months under the overpass with Jake before he could shut off the nightmare memories, the sick stomach, the fear.

An hour later they were sitting at the coffee shop, trying to have a good time. *That's what friends do*, Gerald thought. *Friends share secrets*. Regan, her tongue loosened chemically, babbled about her sickeningly perfect little brother whom she hated, and her father's angry, red face, his cutting words when her report card came in June. And her mother's ugly tears. That was the worse, she complained. "Mothers have no right to cry when they're angry. I'd rather be yelled at." She sucked noisily at the straw in her Frappuccino. "Crying makes a kid feel really guilty but it doesn't change anything."

Gerald guessed it was his turn to confide. "My mom never cried. She just got drunk or high and if she got mad at me, she swore and tried to hit me. Then she would pass out."

"God."

"I left. She didn't care."

Regan leaned forward, ready to hear more. "Was it horrible, being on the street? Like where did you sleep, in doorways or under bushes? God."

Gerald didn't want to talk about it anymore. He stood up and pulled on his jacket. "Yes, I wouldn't advise it, no matter how pissy your little brother is."

He was tired of trying to make a friend. "Let's go. We'll miss the movie." He hadn't used in weeks and he felt twitchy, like he had to be careful not to let the pot take over, make him say stuff he didn't want to say.

After a minute, Regan caught up with him and they walked without talking towards the bus stop. She seemed to be pouting and confirmed it when she finally said, "We could have gone to the next show, you know. Stayed a while longer in the park enjoying the rocks."

Gerald never wanted to see that park again, but he knew he would soon.

The movie cured Regan's pout about not staying longer at the bench. Gerald understood movies can do that, make you forget what you're angry about, take you to a place where the problems are someone else's to solve and they usually are and you begin to believe what's bothering you isn't so bad after all. They ended up laughing over coffee and dishes of ice cream, mostly about how stupid their teachers had been their sophomore year and the times they escaped to the restrooms or a back hall to smoke and laugh with other smokers.

"Did you have a girl friend?" Regan asked as she licked her spoon and pushed the dish aside.

Gerald could answer truthfully. "My mom moved us around a lot. I never had a chance to get to know many people, guys or girls." He didn't mention that the motels and the shelters didn't lend themselves to having friends over, and his own appearance probably discouraged the few people who might have been friendly, the not-popular ones, but who gave him a friendly kind of look even though his jeans were dirty and he probably stank. Or about his own fantasies. "How about you?"

"I had a few. Even in grade school. I grew boobs early and boys looked at them and tried to touch them when we passed in the hall. They made remarks that made the other girls jealous. Some of them stuffed toilet paper in their baby bras to compete. I thought it was fun to be popular with the boys and occasionally a brave kid would ask me to go with him."

"Go? Where?"

"Nowhere, actually. It was a way of saying we were going steady but most of the parents wouldn't allow real dates, alone. Going with me was a big deal to those wimpy little seventh graders. I let a couple of them have a quick feel in the janitor's room and made their reputations as lovers really soar." Regan grinned at the memory. "But by high school it was more than a feel. You know about all that I'm sure."

Gerald knew. More than a feel happened to him often, only not with anyone he was attracted to. Memories flashed of dark motel rooms, alcohol fumes, her mother's "Hey, he's just a kid," as drunken groan and a weight descended on him. He had filed those scenes somewhere far away. He asked, "Yeah, so did you have real boyfriends then?" He was curious to learn what normal kids do if they like someone. He had never really liked someone.

"Sure. A different one every week for a while. The popular girls began to talk about me, and voted me out of the stupid sorority they had." When Regan noticed his frown, she explained. "A secret club. For popular girls. They met after school at each other's houses, drank beer and smoked pot in the backyards and lied to their parents about their rituals. 'Smells strange because we burn incense,' I heard one of them tell her mother and the mother said, 'Sounds good.' Then they had a secret meeting without me and informed me by a note that I was no longer a member. I had a slutty reputation."

So that's what normal high school is like. Maybe I should be glad I hadn't made any friends in the three high schools I went to. "The only person I could have called a friend at one of my schools was a teacher who seemed interested in me. She asked questions. I wanted to trust her and I answered them. A few weeks later, a social worker took me out of class and asked if it were true, that my mother and I lived in a motel and men visited my mother and drank. 'And what else?' she asked, and I knew I had to lie."

"'I told her, 'Nothing else. The men were our friends. They brought us liquor sometimes. That's all.' I lied because I knew if I said more to this woman with worry lines denting her forehead, I'd be taken away from my mother. A foster home sounded much worse than a motel room with someone who loved me. At least she said she loved me and I believed her."

Gerald had never talked to anyone like this before. "I don't believe most people who say they want to help me. They just want to control me, make me be like them."

Regan didn't seem shocked by his story. "Yeah, like my parents. I told them the truth and I ended up at Grandma Betsy's house instead of Europe."

"Why?

"According to my mother, my sluttiness got me pregnant. She didn't say sluttiness, of course. She said I had made a bad decision, and they would help me survive it. I would get an abortion, spend the summer thinking about what happened, and make a plan for not letting it or anything else get in the way of my becoming a strong woman. That's the way my parents talk. They couldn't imagine I'd made ten, maybe more, bad decisions that year and they didn't ask. So, I'm here at my Grandma's, thinking over one of them. I don't know who got me pregnant, but I think it was Alex who promised to pull out and didn't, the creep."

"No condom? No pill?"

"Other bad decisions I hope I won't make again. And next fall I will be going to a private school away from home. My parents have had it with me, even though they don't know the half of it." Regan's finger wiped across an eyelid. Gerald wondered if she was feeling angry or sad. Gerald would be sad. He *was* sad. He'd lost a mother and maybe soon a grandmother. Maybe Regan was sad, too, for the same reasons, only she might not realize it yet.

"Shit. I hate my parents."

He said something like that a few days ago too. And now he wasn't so sure.

They left the ice cream store and decided to walk home. Each of them, Gerald realized, was glad they'd found someone to talk to, about real life, not about cleaning closets and whatever Regan and her grandmother talked about. Maybe about condoms and pills if Grandma Betsy could hear the anger in her granddaughter.

They'd walked about a mile when a familiar figure stood in their way, hands on his hips, shaking his head. "Moon, aren't you supposed to be home planning a little gig for next week?"

"Fuck you, Jake," Gerald said. Maybe having a friend next to him made him brave enough raise his voice, but Jake only shrugged.

"No, Moon. You want to treat me nice, remember? We've got a plan and you will follow it if you want to keep on living." The grinning bully paused as he turned his attention and his gaze on Regan. "Another lost-soul-living-with-a-rich-grandma? Moon knows what I mean." He moved towards Regan. "Nice," he said.

"And who are you again?" Regan asked, smug, flirting.

"He's only a guy, from. . .around here." Gerald pulled on Regan's arm but she didn't move. "Let's go.'

"No, this is interesting. Don't be a shit. Introduce us."

"Jake, Regan." Gerald stepped back and watched the dance the two fell into as they took each other in. They liked what they saw, and Jake threw an arm over Regan's shoulders.

"Nice to meet you," he smirked.

"Of course, Jake.'"

Still with his arm round her shoulders, Jake said, "Let me walk you home." And before Gerald could object, Regan moved closer to him and started walking, glancing over his arm, signaling Gerald to follow them with her head.

They left Regan at Grandma Betsy's, Jake writing with a ball-point pen on his arm the telephone number she gave him. "My cell," she said as she walked up the pathway to the door.

"See ya, new girl."

Gerald didn't like what just happened. "Jake, what are you doing?"

Jake wiped a palm across his sprouts of greasy hair. "Always helps to have an extra hand in a job. She looks like a player."

"She doesn't know shit about what you're planning. She's a girl who is in detention because her parents didn't like what she'd been doing, which was not anything close to what you are doing."

"Next Friday, Moon. We'll talk before then to make sure you've done your part."

He sauntered away, his usual smirk twisting his lips, as Gerald arrived at Alicia's walk and when he opened the door, he could smell pizza.

A half hour later, Alicia answered the phone and called, "It's for you, Gerald. A girl?" She sounded pleased.

"He's really hot." Regan whispered into her phone. "You know what he did? When he left me, he slipped a blue pill into my pocket. Oxy, he said. Does that mean he likes me?"

"Regan, be careful. Jake is really bad news, worse than anyone you ever banged in high school. He. . ."

"I love bad boys, Gerald. I can handle him. You'll see."

10

ALICIA

"Wonder how our grandkids got along," Betsy says as she leans forward to let me out of her car. "Don't hear any sirens, so I guess okay."

"Can't get into trouble in a movie house unless Mad Max inspires them to get violent." I bend into the open car window and realize I really mean it when I thank Betsy for the afternoon. "Perhaps we can do this again, an art fair lunch, or maybe just a lunch?"

Betsy grins. "Hope so. Gerald is maybe the quiet kind of kid Regan needs. We should promote their friendship even if it damages your grandson." I try to laugh, but I think about the damage Gerald may have already experienced. It's not the right time to bring it up. Betsy drives away and I walk up to my front door. The house is quiet. Gerald must still be at the movie. I look in the fridge and wonder what we'll eat for dinner. Maybe Mac and Cheese. It has no eyes.

A little quiet nap, that's what I need. And a moment to reflect how much I enjoyed being out, looking at lovely things, talking to a cheerful woman over a glass of wine. When had I decided the solace of a book and an empty calendar would bring peace? It does, of course, along with questions I don't want to think about in the middle of the night, questions that have no answers. *Why am I alive?* for instance. *I could disappear, for all the world cares, for all I care.* Depressive thoughts. When they rise like drowned corpses in a murky lake of angst, I turn on the light and hide in a book for an hour or so until my eyes close, force the morbid questions to go under until the next time.

At this moment, tired as I am, the only thoughts I have are about dinner tonight, what shall we do tomorrow, does Gerald need a smart phone, should I spend time with Mad Max to discover how he escapes whatever is on his mind?

No sleep right now. I need to change back to the sweatshirt and pants I wear when I clean. My closet nearly empty now needs a good vacuuming. The carpet will come later when I've gotten rid of the piles of clothes on the floor. On my chest of drawers, I see the jewelry box I've left out. The latch is not hooked. Did I leave it like that?

When I open the box, all the things inside seem just as I left them, except for the ruby earrings which I still have on my ears. But the latch. . .

Confused, I drift into the dining room, and see that the cupboard holding the silver in the buffet is not completely closed. I would not have left it like that, door ajar. Would I?

No. I wouldn't. Someone has been in the house, perhaps when we both were gone. I remember having to use my key to get in, so the door was locked. I had been reluctant to give Gerald a key as I left this morning, but neither of us was sure who would get home first and I didn't want to have him sitting for hours on the porch. He might have left for some reason, for a walk, possibly, then come back, leaving the door unlocked for a while. I check the house. Nothing is missing that I can tell, even the few dollars in the grocery money jar. A mystery. Maybe I'm going crazy. I used to have a friend who often said that about herself. Now I know what she meant.

Crazy or not, I go back to the bedroom, take off the earrings, and move the jewelry box to the drawer holding a few pieces of my own jewelry and my underwear. I shove the box under my emergency incontinence pads. I used to hide my valuables in the pocket of my suitcase containing my Kotex, thinking a thief would be embarrassed to plow through a pile of napkins. I still got robbed, I recall, despite the precautions, in an airport in Johannesburg. Now I'm told people use suitcase keys and wrap their luggage in layers of plastic. Probably works as well as Kotex.

On the way home the other day, on Betsy's recommendation, I bought a half-baked, cheese pizza, mushroom, tomato, and I have the oven hot enough to bake it. I believe meals should have some green in them, so I open a can of green beans and am ready to fry up some bacon to pep them up when I remember that bacon has eyes. Or did. I switch to hazel nuts, chopped, and sit down to the newspaper and a glass of white wine. It has been a good day, but Gerald has disappeared. I tell myself not to worry. Who knows? I'm new at this.

I hear his voice outside, another voice, too, a familiar one: the person who calls, the person who bothers Gerald. Should I go out? Before I make up my mind, Gerald comes through the door, sees me and seems to be wearing a Happy Face, like the graffiti I see on mailboxes, just for me. Now I am worried.

"Hi, Alicia! I had a good time and I hope you did too." Gerald doesn't quite hug me but he moves in and touches my arm as he hands me the key. "You probably want this back."

"Yes. Did you need it when you went out earlier?"

Gerald frowns. "I didn't go out until I left with Regan. Oh, yes, I did. She wanted to see the park, so we walked over and talked for a little."

"Did you lock the door when you left? I always do."

"Sorry, I didn't think. . . we were so close, you know, didn't dawn on me." Gerald's eyes meet mine. "Won't happen again. And I did lock up when we headed out for the movie."

He seems to be telling the truth, about leaving. I'm thinking I should tell him that I suspect someone has been in the house. Something about the way he's looking at me makes me not say anything. Perhaps he's just hungry.

"Any fruit? We only ate popcorn for lunch." He finds an apple in the basket on the counter, bites into it, moans with satisfaction. "Just what I need. How was your day?"

The hundreds of mystery novels that I've escaped into over the years have taught me one thing: a person who is lying will look you straight in the eyes. Just as he is doing right now. "Fine," I answer. "How was the movie today?"

"Terrific. Very noisy, very exciting. I love Charlize Theron. What do I smell, pizza?"

He's not talking about what I want to talk about. "Yes, pizza." I need to get some answers. "Who were you talking to just now?" I peek at the pizza into the oven as I ask and Gerald is walking away from me, heading for his bedroom. I follow him. "Gerald, who were you talking to?"

At his door, he turns. The Happy Face has become a Mad Face, if there is such a thing. He looks at me straight on and says, "Shit, Alicia, you aren't in charge of me. A friend, that's all." He closes the door and leaves me speechless.

"Pizza will be ready in eight minutes." That's all I can think of saying.

I'm slicing the pizza into triangles when he comes back into the kitchen. "Sorry. I've got some stuff on my mind and I'm not good at hiding it." He lifts several triangles onto a plate and watches as I do the same. "Let's just sit here at the counter. It's easier to reach for more from here." He pulls up a stool for himself and one for me.

I eat at the counter only at breakfast. My arm touches his as I settle next to him.

I take a bite, let the cheese drip to my chin, chew, find the courage to ask, "What stuff, Gerald?" We're so close I must turn my body to look at his face. He's blinking, his eyes moist, red. I don't say any more, but his tears surprise me. I didn't know teenaged boys cried. Of course, I did comfort a weeping husband more than once. But I knew why the tears back then. But as Gerald has indicated, this is none of my business.

We chew in silence. Gerald uses his paper napkin on my chin and on his eyelids.

I can't stand the silence. "I worry about you."

"Don't, please, I can handle it." Then he gives me that Happy

Face smile again, unconvincing because his eyes are still wet. It's my turn to get angry. I take his elbow, make him sit back down again.

"I know you are a strong young man. You must be to have lived the life I'm imagining you've had. But even strong people need to ask for help, or for advice, or for whatever else they need occasionally."

He pulls his arm away and one of his pizza-sticky hands covers his eyes. "You don't know what you are talking about."

"No, I don't. You must help me. It's that dirty boy, isn't it? The one who has been coming by, watching you. Has he said something, threatened you?" I can imagine it, a bully like that saying whatever is that's making Gerald so upset. I should go out and find him, tell him he cannot go around frightening others. Or I'll call the police. "What is his name?"

Gerald blows his nose in his napkin, wads it up, drops it on his plate. Then he picks it up, stuffs it into his pocket. "Sorry," he murmurs.

I break into what might be hysterical laughter.

Gerald looks at me, startled. "What?"

"You are so worried that you are close to tears but you stop in mid-sentence to pick up the snotty napkin you know I won't want you to leave on your plate. Gerald, I don't give a damn about the napkin at this moment. I care about you." The words come without me directing them, as if they have been waiting to be let loose. I touch his arm again, this time not to lead him somewhere, but only to touch him.

Gerald looks away. "Jake," he says. "He has been saying rotten things to me and about me. He wants to pay me back for not being his friend any more. I don't think he means what he's saying. . .he's. . .strange, like he isn't quite all there. I'm not really afraid, just sick of him." Gerald sends me his blue-eyed gaze. "I care about you, too, Alicia. I'm glad you are my grandmother."

There he goes again. Now is not the time to correct him, but we do have to get that whole grandma thing straightened out. I wouldn't mind if I were his grandmother, but somewhere he has received some untruthful information. Maybe he does have a real grandmother somewhere, someone who may be looking for him. Not very caring of me to hope he doesn't.

Gerald is no longer blinking, and I suggest we see what's on TV before we head to bed, to kind of pull ourselves together. We have a big day coming up, I remind him. Shops, Goodwill, maybe even lunch. I'll need him to help me schlep the bags and hangers into the car, in to the stores and shops, and finally to Goodwill. "And along the way, I'll depend on you to help me park," I warn him. "I have right-side-of-the-car dyslexia."

First, I'll get my robe and slippers on in case the show we watch puts me to sleep or close to it. I have another reason for going into my bedroom. I have something I will look at for the first time in twenty years or more, hidden in the bottom drawer of my dresser. I take out the black bag, reach in, and take out the handgun Fred bought just before he died. He had been worried about a series of break-ins in the neighborhood, and he and I took some lessons on how to load it, aim it, and fire it, all of which we did a few times on a firing range. Then the burglar was caught and the gun went into my drawer, forgotten until this moment.

I'll be ready if Jake the Crazy Person tries to enter my house, tries to hurt the almost-grandson I've come to be glad about. I hope I remember how to load it. First I need to find the ammunition.

I also need to find a good place to keep it, the gun. Under a pillow? Not handy for daytimes threats. In my bra? Amongst my flat girls something hard would protrude and announce itself. In my purse? Again, not handy. I find my old Playtex girdle and tug until it goes over my flabby hips and surrounds my equally flabby waist. The gun settles in amongst the flab, poking at my intestines only when I bend over. This will work once I'm sure how to load it. I try not to imagine what would happen to my lower parts if a loaded pistol goes off inside my girdle. I'll give it a try. We have some other things to take care of tomorrow.

First, the Goodwill clothes. And it felt so good to empty closets that I walk around the living room to see what else we can get rid of. I'm suddenly struck with the reality that I've not looked at what has been lining the walls of this room and the dining room for years. Pictures that Fred chose, hung. They seemed okay at the time, thirty years ago. Now they bore me. Prints, landscapes, engravings that no longer have any meaning to me.

I go back to the kitchen, pour a glass of wine, stand in front of the window. The view outside, lit with soft floodlights, is alive with growth: trees, rhodies, lilacs, and in the shady spots, green, blooming hostas. A month from now the scene will be completely transformed, and chrysanthemums and asters will fill in the spots the other plants have deserted. A lively scene. I know why the art in the front rooms doesn't touch me. It's static, has been for more than twenty years. Time for a change.

When we were first married, Fred and I used to visit art galleries on Saturdays after the monthly openings of local shows. Sometimes when we both agreed on a painting or a sculptural piece we'd buy it and feel quite pleased with ourselves and our good taste. Good taste was important to both of us. When we had friends in, we directed their attentions to our latest acquisitions and waited for the compliments. One time a friend I grew to dislike suggested that our art took the place of children. "Both are expensive," she added, "and it takes years to be sure of their worth in one's life. At least you can sell art if you end up not liking it." She thought she was being very clever but I remember turning away, excusing myself to tend to the dinner. Now I'm beginning to agree with the woman. What does one do with art that has little meaning anymore? Sell it?

Then we watch TV for a while and during an ad for Victoria's Secret bras which I mute but don't turn off, Gerald looks at me and asks, "Where are those earrings you had on today? They were nice. I've never seen you wear jewelry before."

"I put them away. Some place they are safe."

Gerald nods. "Guess they are valuable?"

"I suppose so. I really don't know. They were my mother-in-law's. I inherited them when Fred died. She didn't want me to have them, but I got them anyway. But I don't wear them often. I've been thinking of selling them and some other things she had. Don't know quite how to do that. Most of the stuff is antique."

"I hope you have them hidden in a good spot. You never know. . ."

"Yes, I do, but maybe we can look for a shop that buys old jewelry tomorrow, along with the consignment shops. If you want to."

"Sure. Let's do it. I'll look in the telephone book for addresses."

Gerald seems very enthusiastic about the search. I'm now sure he has seen the jewelry box, has looked at its contents. Maybe he wants to know where to sell the collection after he's stolen it? Apparently, one open latch has turned me into a paranoiac, ugly, disappointed old bitch. I am so sorry. I had harbored a few small hopeful dreams about what might come of all this change.

The phone rings and I answer it in my bedroom. If it is the scummy young man who has been hanging around, I'll tell him to— what? Fuck off? Never have said those words aloud, thought them a couple of times, maybe this time? I check the caller identity.

"Hello, Betsy. What's up? Another art show?"

"I'm just checking in. Mostly to let you know that I found a bag of what looks like marijuana in Regan's pocket just now and I'm wondering if it has any connection with our kids' play date today."

"What does Regan say?"

"I haven't asked her yet. Thought maybe you found some evidence of using around your house? Doobies, I think they call them."

"Doobies?"

"Joints. Pot cigarettes"

"No doobies yet, Betsy." I hesitate and I don't tell her about my own swarming suspicions. "Is this what I'm in for? A new vocabulary?"

"Yep. Until the child is about thirty-two. Then mothers and grandmas can relax. It's out of their hands at that point and only a good lover can take over."

"You read romance novels, don't you? I suspect they are easier on a parent than mysteries. At least gory crimes aren't usually laid on the kids."

"You are fussing about something else. Want to share?"

"What I'm fussing about will indicate that I'm one step into senility. I'll share when I am clear what I'm fussing about." I hesitate, glad I may have a chance to do that. "As far as Regan goes, I'd let her know you know and see what happens. Many years ago, a friend said that her daughter had brought pot to a family picnic and when it was discovered, my friend gathered everyone around the campfire, grandparents included, and asked her daughter to roll a joint and pass it around the circle. She did. Everyone inhaled, grinned, and forgave the girl. She never brought marijuana anywhere near her family again. Maybe you need to ask Regan to share. Or not. What do I know?"

With that, we say, "Let's talk again soon," and I hang up.

"That's a funny story, Alicia," Gerald says, standing at my door. "Regan needs that kind of mother—or grandmother."

How can I doubt a young man who could say that?

Easy, Fred says.

What do you know, smartass? I answer.

Feisty old lady.

I hear him laugh for some reason. I feel better.

11

GERALD

The TV movies were not all that great. Gerald yawned and told Alicia he was going to bed.

"Thank God, I've been ready for a half hour. Do they always have to end up wrestling in bed? Besides," Alicia added, "we have a big day tomorrow."

"Yeah," Gerald agreed. "I like to laugh every once in a while. Or be scared. Sex is not that interesting to me." *Never has been*, Gerald thought, *maybe never will be*. He picked up his discarded shoes.

They turned off the TV and said goodnight in the hall. Gerald needed to pee before he went into his room, but Alicia had her own bathroom in her bedroom and had disappeared after a flutter of fingers at her door.

I could get used to living like this, Gerald told himself as he brushed his teeth.

TV, clean sink, pizza regularly, someone I might be able to trust. If only he could convince Alicia that she was his grandmother, it might keep going, this good life. But first he had to get rid of Jake. Maybe the scumball would be satisfied with what he finds in this house and leave him alone when it was all over. He rinsed his mouth, inspected his teeth. Jake satisfied? With Jake, there was always more to want.

Ready for bed in a T-shirt, he pulled back the covers and felt under the pillow. It was still there, the diary. Gerald opened it, knowing that only a few pages were written on, his mother never able to finish a project, even raising a son. But she had described a little about her own childhood, days on a farm, her mother Alice who had left her baby daughter with her parents Sonja and Drummond and went looking for that baby's father. She never came back. For a while, Grandma Sonja and Grandpa Peder kept the baby they named Gretchen, a name from the old country, for a few years.

"I lived with them long enough for me to learn to love them and the farm with its chickens and pigs," his mother had written. *"Then Grandpa died. Grandma Sonja got sick with cancer and couldn't keep me—or the farm.*

"The Graysons, friends from church, childless, adopted me." Jessie's pencil eraser had smudged some of her words. Or the smears might have been tears, Gerald thought as he reread the page. *"They wanted to help me begin again. They gave me a new name, Jessie, after an aunt I never ever met. And my last name was changed to Grayson.*

"I never did like my new name and I didn't like my new parents. More than once I ran away to Grandma Sonja's little apartment and begged her to take me back. But she died. I had a vanished mother and a dead grandma and two people who called themselves my parents but who weren't. I was fifteen when I ran away for the last time and began looking for my real mother."

On the inside of the back cover of the diary someone had printed, "To my sweet granddaughter, who I know as Gretchen, on her birthday. Write on these pages as your life gets better and better. Grandma Sonja."

Not so better and better, Gerald thought, as he deciphered the faint words. He flipped through the blank pages that followed the first paragraphs that were probably written during the days or months Jessie lived on the run still looking for her mother. She hadn't found her. Drugged, anxious years followed until, she told Gerald, she met a red-haired construction worker and a baby was born and the three of them became a family. When he disappeared, Jessie and one-year-old Gerald were on their own. Because

"Mama" reminded Jessie of her own vanished mother, she told a young Gerald to call her by her first name.

From the stories Jessie had told him, and what he remembered even if he didn't want to, Gerald understood that his mother had found drugs and men instead of a mother during those angry years. Sometimes Jessie worked and tried to be a good mother of the little boy she had named Gerald after no one. She just liked the name, she told her son during one of these calm times. "Don't ever change it," she said, her fingers playing with his red curls. "You'll always be Gerald."

Once, on a sober day, Jessie showed the diary to Gerald and tore out a page and wrote her mother's name on it. "My mother, your grandma," she said, handing the note to Gerald. "If you need someone and I'm not around. I couldn't find her. Maybe you can." Gerald kept the paper. Later he would take it out of his pack and say the name aloud. He could almost hear Jessie's voice, the voice she had used when she loved her son.

Gerald had first read his mother's diary on a cold bench a few days after he took it from the table in the motel, just after he closed the door on the life into which Jessie had dragged him. Tucked deep into the back cover of the book, he had discovered several yellowed and folded papers. He had returned them, unread, into the diary.

He pulled the coverlet over his knees, leaned against a pillow, and stuck his fingers into the loose binding of the back cover. The crinkled papers' edges clung to the crack at the last page, and caught on his fingernails. He slid them out and opened them. **Birth Certificate**, one read. *Alice Drummond was born on May, 1947, to Sonja Dubrinski and Peder Drummond in St. Anthony Hospital in Redlands, Oregon.* The second paper, **Adoption Certificate**, certified the legal adoption of Gretchen Drummond, to be known hereafter as Jessie Grayson, born in 1972 to birth parent Alice Drummond. Adoptive parents were Theodore and Katherine Grayson. The certificate was dated 1978.

The most important name on the certificate was Alice Drummond, the name his mother had written down on that torn sheet of paper. When the overpass became a hellhole of drugs and pain and a pimp named Jake, Gerald remembered of Jessie's quest and he searched for that grandmother. He found her on Google in the county library. Alicia Drummond.

Shit. He should have looked further into the corners of Google for Alice. Perhaps because Alicia Drummond turned out to be a successful director of a local pipe company, he had stopped looking.

Alice Drummond. Alicia Drummond. Gerald found his notepad and pencil in his backpack and tried doing the math. Was it possible that the Alice from the certificate was Alicia? She would be sixty-eight. That seemed right. Gerald tore off a clean sheet of paper and kept scribbling. If his mother Jessie was born when Alice was twenty-five, in 1972, then Jessie would have had him, Gerald, in 2000, when she was twenty-eight. And Gerald was fourteen, almost fifteen, in 2015.

My age. Maybe Alicia changed her name to sound more business like when she got her job in an office.

It all fit. The numbers added up.

The clock showed 11:15, probably too late to contact the only person Gerald knew who had a computer. Regan had given him her cell phone number, though, and might still be up Facebooking or whatever. Gerald searched his pockets, found the slip of paper and guessed that the best place to talk would be on the back deck, if Alicia's phone cord reached that far. He crept out of his room, made sounds as if he were going into the bathroom, and picked up the phone in the kitchen. The cord stretched through the doorway and Gerald shut the door as much as he could before he dialed. Moments later, Regan's perky voice asked, "Hi, what's up? I can't hear you," and Gerald whispered, "I need for you to Google a name for me." He spelled it.

"Your grandma?"

"Maybe. Just don't stop at Alicia; continue until maybe you find an Alice Drummond. I'll hang on. That is, if you aren't busy right now."

"Are you kidding? I'm in a coma. This sounds exciting."

Ten minutes later, "I'm back."

"And?"

"Found Alicia Drummond. She's in Portland, retired, deceased husband, no children. She retired after a long career as an office manager in a pipe company. But that's not all. I also looked up Alice."

"Found her way deep in the Drummond listings, in the obituaries. Alice Drummond, formerly of Gresham, died ten years ago at the age of fifty-eight. She had been a waitress at the Imperial Hotel for twenty years. Her only relative, a cousin, Fredrick Drummond, preceded her in death ten years before."

"Fred? Her cousin? Dead? What does that mean?"

"She's been dead for ten years. Is that a problem?"

"Only that I don't have a grandma anymore."

"My grandma's a bitch. She's grounded me for three days for nothing "

"Like?"

"I borrowed a little of her whiskey for my Coke tonight. God."

"See you in a day or so. And thanks, I guess."

12

ALICIA

I open the phone book, look up art/auctions. Several companies are listed and I write the numbers down. The person who answers my first call, when he hears of the Japanese woodblock prints and several artists' names, tells me he would love to look at what I have and give me an idea of their value at an auction.

"I'd like to drop by your place first. This afternoon?" I suggest, and I set a time.

Gerald is standing at the door. "You are selling the painting? The one in the living room with the long road?"

I hear the disappointment in his voice. "I didn't know you liked it. Maybe not that one."

"I hope not. Are we ready for Goodwill and wherever else?"

"Give me a half hour to make sure I've got everything." I've just been struck with an idea, a very unexpected one, one that bloomed at the mention of the painting Gerald likes. I shut my bedroom door, sit on the edge of the bed, and try to make sense of what I'm about to consider.

It feels like it's been a very long road collecting this old stuff. Not only clothes and art but the years of chosen isolation in this house. If I sell off the remnants of the past thirty years, the clothes, the art, surely, I can get rid of other unwanted parts of my life also, beginning with my lonely house. Gerald could move with me to a nice condo, go to a good school, become the young man he wants to be. No, that I want him to be, I realize. I'll have to allow Gerald to make his own decisions about his future, but wouldn't it be easier for him to do so from a solid foundation of education and, I almost think "love," but don't, instead, someone who cares about him?

The consignment shops and Goodwill will be the first stops. Then the auction house. Then a realtor. I bend to push myself up from my chair and feel pain in my lower stomach. I reach into the girdle and remove the pistol. Getting out of the Playtex girdle takes a little longer, but I return both to the bottom drawer in my dresser. I won't need either for today's excursions. I do need to find the ammunition for the gun and I'm not sure where we put it twenty years ago. Gerald's not up yet so I can look around without explaining what I'm looking for. I know it's not in my chest of drawers. Only the black gun bag is hiding under a rubber girdle. Perhaps Fred had hidden the box, now that I remember what it looked like, somewhere else.

We have gone through the closet quite thoroughly. I open the closet door, push aside the empty hangers. Only the sealed storage case with the fox jacket inside it hangs at the end of the rod. I haven't worn the jacket for twenty-five years, a bit intimidated after an acquaintance's mink was soaked in blood or something by protesters in front of the opera house. Not that my jacket is as valuable as a mink coat, but I couldn't face the idea of being on the front page of the *Oregonian* like my friend was, dripping red paint onto the sidewalk. Most of us stopped wearing real fur and established our status by wearing designer gowns under politically correct wraps. Except about then Fred died and I moved on for a bit to a sports car and wind-blown hair. Fred would have been either appalled or loved me those few years of my emancipation. I am now, both, just thinking of them.

The box is heavy. When I lift it off the hanger, it nearly takes me to the floor along with it. The case contains something more than a fox jacket. I sit down and look for its zipper tag and discover it is secured with a suitcase lock. Well, I have a screwdriver to take care of that problem. I just need to get over to the chest of drawers to find it. I crawl on my hands and knees until I reach the bed and then pull myself upright. I'm not sure if this maneuver is more graceful or less than the camel-rising maneuver I often use in similar situations. I'm glad no one is watching, except perhaps my ghostly Fred, who has not interfered, probably appalled again.

The screwdriver and my battering the lock with its handle are successful. The case opens. The jacket smells like mothballs, and it seems to be shedding, hairs floating as I touch it. At the bottom, under the jacket, I find the box of ammunition and a bit of Fred. His toys. Until this moment, I have not been not aware he had toys. These probably accompanied him to San Francisco or were played with the nights I was away at conferences or taking a break at the beach without him. Fred's toys included a vibrator, a larger one than my own, with heavy batteries. And a few devices that seemed designed to pinch sensitive pieces of skin. And for some reason, a roll of decorated Mickey Mouse tape. And two VCR tapes and three illustrated books. And a box of condoms, a precaution that came too late for Fred, but not for those who may have shared the toys with him.

A tsunami of sadness rolls over me, forces my head down to my knees, takes the breath from me. Not sadness for myself. For Fred, for the lie he felt forced to live his life by, for the toys he had to hide from me. "Dear Fred, you were born forty years too soon. I'm so sorry for you," I tell him as I put everything back in the box except the bullets. I will give it all, the fur jacket, the toys, to Goodwill. Someone may be able to use them.

"Even the jacket, I bet," Fred suggests.

Camel-rising, this time. I stand up, drag the storage box to the other piles of clothes waiting for Goodwill. I don't allow myself to think about Gerard. I tuck the container of ammunition in the drawer close to the gun in case I ever need either of them.

13

GERALD

Gerald woke up, remembered with a thud that Alicia was no longer his grandmother. Never was. He was back where he started, under the overpass. But Alicia never believed she was Gerald's grandmother and she still took him in and fed him and acted the way Gerald believed grandmothers acted. Maybe she suspected she might be and just in case, decided to be nice to him. Whatever. Gerald could not imagine going back to what he had run away from. He could not admit the realities of that life to Alicia. Alicia would kick him out and he would return to the overpass. If she knew he was helping Jake steal from her the same would happen. The only solution he could come up with, as he lay awake for what seemed like all night, was to keep everything going as it had been, he insisting he had proof that Alicia was his grandmother and doing what Jake demanded he do. Alicia would get robbed and maybe, if it went okay, she wouldn't suspect he was involved. Gerald could keep living with her. Afterward he would tell Alicia the truth, about Alice Drummond, at least. Not the other stuff.

He pushed back against his pillow and lay making a list in his head what he and Alicia were about to do, tomorrow, just one week before Jake would demand his report and would carry out his plan. First, they would sell the clothes and find the nearest Goodwill for the items that consignment stores don't want. Then they would look for antique shops, and he'd ask Alicia to bring at least the earrings, maybe all the jewelry, to see if it's valuable enough to get rid of before Jake stole it. If it was, Alicia would get the money, Jake wouldn't.

At breakfast, though, Alicia had another plan. "As you know, I have some art, mostly Fred's, that no longer speaks to me. Maybe we can expand our search today to a few more galleries."

Alicia led Gerald through the living room and pointed to a painting over the fireplace. Gerald didn't like it much, too brown, sad, only a rabbit in one corner to give it life. He liked the owl on a limb more than the rabbit. Then Alicia told him what it might be worth, the well-known artist now showing in New York galleries. "Wow," he said, "I can't believe anyone would pay twenty-two thousand dollars for that." A person could buy a great car for that money.

In the dining room, a room in which Gerald hadn't spent much time, a group of five small black and white and red pictures of, he thought, snowy scenes on roads, hung as a group, boring until Alicia pointed at the red graffiti in the corners of each picture. "This is the way Japanese woodblock artists identify their work. Fred loved the serenity of the prints. I did too."

They walked down the hall, paused. "We bought this when the artist was just beginning, but I never liked it much. Seemed too dark. Now he's also famous." Gerald stopped in front of the painting, the long road painting. A highway, yellow lines in the middle, climbed over a curving hill, through a green-black forest, into a blue/gray sky. This picture he could understand. "That's like me," he said. "On a road to a place with a little more light."

Alicia glanced at him. "You're a mystery, boy. Who are you, really? I mean it. You need to tell me, over this morning's Cheerios—about the road you are on."

At the kitchen counter Gerald noticed that Alicia had sometime in the past few days bought rice milk. No eyes involved. He wasn't sure any more about the no eyes rule, nor about much else. He would not tell Jake about the art, how valuable it was. He crunched through the cereal and stirred the strawberry yogurt. Does rice milk make yogurt? Does it matter? Alicia sat watching him, waiting.

"I'm don't know who I am, Alicia. I don't know where I'm going. I do remember a mother holding me, singing, a mother not talking to me, a mother screaming at me, men either being nice to me, or not, telling me to go away, grabbing me and shoving me into a dark place where I curled up and wondered where I was." And other stuff she didn't need to know, like how scared he had been. He put down his spoon. "But it wasn't all bad. Mom got sober once in a while and she and I would sleep together and tell stories and snuggle and I guess it was these times that kept me hoping. For what, I wasn't sure." He held the bowl up to his mouth and swallowed a satisfying last mouthful of eyeless milk.

"I ran away from my mom, left her unconscious, vomiting. I had to leave to save myself. I went back a day or so later to check on her and the motel manager told me she had overdosed. 'Dead, probably,' he said. 'A hard way to escape paying her rent.'" Gerald glanced at his bowl. It was empty. "Her name was on the obituary list in The *Oregonian* a week later."

"Tragic." Alicia closed her eyes. "So where did you go?"

"I met a kid who said that I could find a place to sleep under the overpass on First Street. He'd been doing it, and it was safe if I avoided the druggies. I went, found a spot, and after a few hours met Jake. I told you about him. He loaned me an old dog, a piece of cardboard, and for a while I panhandled." Gerald stopped talking.

"And then you came to my door."

"Because my mom had given me her diary and a note that had your name on it. 'Your grandma,' she said. I never had a chance to ask her more about it."

"The diary under your pillow?"

"You found it?"

"I didn't read it." She glanced at him. "I know you've been in **my** room too."

This is it, Gerald thought. *I'm getting kicked out. I don't blame her.*

"So, we're even. Let's plan tomorrow's day." Alicia got out the telephone book and flipped pages, searching for the addresses of the places they were going to. "Consignment first," she said. "If we can sell it, let's do it."

Gerald felt his eyes blur. "Sure. Let's do it." This was the first time he could remember being forgiven, no strings. For the life in the camp, as much as he had confessed at least, for the STD stuff in the hospital, and for going into a bedroom not his own. How far can Alicia's forgiveness stretch? Not as far as it would need to if Alicia were to learn the whole truth.

He put that thought away. "Maybe a consignment shop would take your earrings, if you want to sell them?"

"Good idea. I'll put the jewelry in my purse. I'll never wear it. But," she added, "would you want it?"

For the second time in a few minutes, Gerald felt the tears rise, catch in his eyelashes. "I don't think so, but thank you." Another lie, but an okay one this time.

"Jake tells me you two have a big plan to get rich." Regan exhaled and a cloud of smoke fogged her face. Gerald wondered if second-hand pot smoke would make him high.

Probably, he thought, remembering the couple of times Jake blew smoke into his mouth and lungs, and he went dizzy. They were hunched behind a couple of lavender bushes in the Betsy's back yard because Regan was sure that the sweet lavender smell would absorb the pot smell.

"What did he say? And when did you see him, for godsake?"

"This morning. That's why I called you."

. "I told you he's really bad news. I'm not kidding."

"He was looking for you. Said he wanted to make sure you've done your part. Next Friday, he said. What's this all about? And do you need a partner? I think Jake likes me." She pulled a plump plastic bag from a pocket. "He gave me this."

Gerald closed his eyes. "What else did he tell you?"

"Only that you and he were going to commit a perfect crime. And your grandmother would be involved." Regan, the joint at her lips, waited a moment, added, "As the victim." She laughed, smoke escaping. "I told him I'd love to do something mean to my own grandma when he's through with yours."

"Not funny, Regan." A dull ache filled Gerald's chest. He had to tell Regan about the plan or she'd never shut up about it. "Jake wants to rob Alicia and he is forcing me to tell him where she keeps things, jewelry, money, and worst of all, he wants the key to the house and the combination to the alarm system." The rims of his eyes burned. "If I don't cooperate, he'll tell Alicia what he and I did at the camp under the overpass. And Alicia will never want to see me again." He wrapped his arms around his legs and folded his head to his knees.

Regan shifted closer to Gerald's huddle. "So, what did you guys do under the overpass?" A breeze of a nasty chuckle floated towards him.

"You wouldn't understand."

"I could try. Maybe I could help. I've had a couple of gay friends and I liked them. And I'm good at getting out of trouble."

Gerald didn't flinch at the words "gay friends," but he couldn't imagine how this girl he barely knew, who didn't know him either, who was stoned and softly crooning "Yesterday" as she wrapped an arm around his shoulders, could possibly help with Jake or in any other way.

"No, thanks. The only thing I can do is disappear before Friday, somewhere where neither Alicia or Jake can find me." He paused for a moment. "Can you lend me some money for a bus ticket?"

Regan's fingers tightened on Gerald's shoulder. "No way. You are the only thing that is keeping me from going nuts around here. And we have a chance for a little excitement. We can do this." She gave him a shake, made Gerald look at her. "Just what do we have to do?"

Despite Jake's comments, Gerald hadn't thought of having Regan as a partner. Maybe? Hope fluttered, made him answer. "We have to get Alicia out of the house on Friday. And I need to give the keys and alarm combination to Jake that morning. And before that, I have to give him the locations of stuff he can steal and sell somewhere."

"And you will need an alibi for the time he's doing all this." Regan shredded the remainder of the butt. "Me." She grinned. "Let's get started."

Betsy found the two of them lounging on the patio and brought them Cokes. "You look like the cats that swallowed a couple of mice," she said. "What are you up to?"

Gerald detected more than curiosity in Betsy's question. This grandmother didn't trust her granddaughter that much. But Regan grinned. "We have a plan. For our grandmas, for being so ready to take two bad teenagers in and giving them a cool summer." She looked at Gerald. "Right? Gerald?"

God, she's good. Gerald managed a "Yep. A plan." A plan? His stomach was beginning to ache.

"We want you and Alicia to go to that spa you've talked about, for a day or longer if you want, and relax. Soaking tubs, massage, lunch. This coming Friday would be a great time to do it. I don't have school that day and Gerald and I can go shopping and do our own kind of relaxing in front of the TV. I want to see *Spectre* and you'd hate it, so we'll go while you are soaking in hot water."

Gerald wasn't convinced that a promise of hot mineral water would get Alicia out of the house next Friday, but he could see that the idea interested Betsy. "And Regan says it's okay with her to lose you for a day," he added, trying to smile.

He also would have liked to lose Regan for a day but it was clear that wasn't going to happen. "Give Alicia a call. I'll let her know you're thinking about the spa. She might want to go, too." It's true that Alicia had changed lately. Easier, if that's a word.

Betsy promised to call, and Gerald walked back to Alicia's, hoping Regan's "This is going to be great," as he left was even partly true. If the plan was to work, he had stuff to do, lists to make, and somehow to get a key. His stomachache eased up as he walked. This crazy idea that had just popped out of Regan's pot-infused brain just might work. Jake might get what he wanted and maybe he would too.

The only person hurt would be Alicia. She'd lose some things, but lately things didn't seem so important to the old woman. She had confessed she was glad to be getting rid of the baggage she'd been dragging around. Gerald had only one piece of baggage and he would never get rid of it, a diary. After Alicia admitted she had seen it, Gerald had hidden the book where Alicia would never look for it, in the pocket of the black suit hanging in Alicia's closet. He hoped no one had died recently enough to need a funeral.

He poured a glass of fake milk, turned. "By the way, Betsy said she was going to phone you about a plan to get away at a spa. Sounds great, and Regan and I go over to Betsy's for the day and get our Netflix craze satisfied."

"I can't imagine going somewhere, even for one day. And what is Netflix? And when?"

"Maybe next Friday? Betsy has that day open and she's sort of interested in getting away—from Regan, I think—for a while."

When Betsy called that evening, Gerald listened as the two women agreed on arrangements for reservations. They planned to be gone one day. Alicia's lips twitched when she explained that Betsy would drive, as if she were either nervous or glad.

Now all Gerald had to do was decide what stuff he would list for Jake. He shut his room's door and got the note pad out of the depths of his backpack and wrote:

1. silver table ware, (buffet in the dining room)
2. what was left of the jewelry after the antique dealer (box in Alicia's room)
3. fur coat in Alicia's closet (in bag)
4. artwork (walls, most of the main rooms)
5. the old vases (on the dining room cabinet)
6. the TV (living room)
7. the 150-year-old antique end table (the end of the sofa)
8. the pills in Alicia's bathroom cabinet
9. Fred's tools, including a large table saw (garage)
10. Fred's vinyl records boxed (on shelves in the garage)
11. And the car (in the garage)

He was sure that was it. He recopied the list so Jake could read it and tore the messy one in half and shoved it in his pocket.

The grandmas would be taking Betsy's car on Friday. Alicia's car would be in the garage, the keys hanging next to the back door because Alicia said she was always losing them if she didn't put them in the same place every time.

The total take: a few hundred dollars, probably, depending on Dougsters's talent for selling on Ebay and his connections with pawnshops, not counting the car. With the car, enough to keep Jake and Dougster in drugs for a while. What else?

Gerald hadn't seen much alcohol, except for white wine, in cupboards. And he didn't know where Alicia kept her cash. Her one credit card was in her purse. Jake may have to do without money until he sold the things he stole. He wouldn't like that.

14

ALICIA

When Betsy calls, she assures me that she's also reluctant to leave the kids alone. "Maybe just part of a day. The place is in the woods, a little hot stream bubbles by the massage rooms and the wooden soaking hot tubs. And it's healthful. Mental health, I'm talking about," she adds. "I need break from teenage hormonal surges. Regan goes from snarky to tears to wild laughter in one sentence. Maybe you feel the same?"

It's been years since I have driven more than just around town. The spa is several hours away down a freeway, across a bridge over the Columbia River. In the woods, Betsy says. I haven't been in a forest since Fred and I, following an old guidebook, went on day hikes. He turned down the corners of pages of the book to keep track of the trails we walked. I laughed that if we kept that up we could travel the distance of the Pacific Coast Trail but only in short spurts, within an hour or two of home. After that, Fred kept a record of our hiking mileage and when we hit a couple hundred miles, he pulled a bottle of pinot noir in his pack and we celebrated on a mossy rock, sprayed by a water fall. By then both Fred and our hiking boots were wearing out. That was our last hike. And I have never had the desire to go into the forests without him.

"Oh, let's do it," Betsy urges. "We don't even have to fix a lunch. They have a small restaurant, only you have to put clothes on to eat there."

"Well, that's an inconvenience. The food had better be good." I am imagining being nude in wooden tub full of hot water that has bubbled out from a spring in the middle of a grove of Doug firs. We'd feel like sprites. Old sprites. "Will you make the reservations?"

"We deserve a really good, expensive lunch, Gerald. You've been very patient." We both had been exhausted on this Saturday after a morning of consignments, Goodwill, and meandering through antique shops. "We may have made some money today."

"Applebee's instead of McDonalds?"

"Much better." We stop for lunch at Aida's where the cloth napkins and table coverings may provide a new experience for Gerald. His hesitation as the server pulls out a chair for me, then his quiet *Wow,* tell me I have guessed right. I'm glad.

We've visited three consignment shops, an antique jewelry shop, a Goodwill, and an auction house where the manager's eager nod indicated he was interested in several paintings and prints hanging on my walls. He will come by on Monday, the day the business is closed, and look at what I have.

The car is almost empty. Only a small bag of plated silver and a couple of gold pieces from the jewelry box weights my purse, but we haven't started looking for new jeans for Gerald, a surprise I had planned for the afternoon. And a shirt, a real shirt, not a T-shirt. "How about dropping into Mario's on Eleventh?" I ask as we finish our coffee. "They have a clothing department for young men, I'm sure"

Gerald's sandwich pauses on the way to his mouth. "Today?"

"We have time." Apparently, he has something else in mind.

"If you want. . . I was thinking about stopping by Regan's, maybe doing something with her. You and I could finish shopping next week when we have more time."

Oh. I keep forgetting that my almost-grandboy is beginning to find a life outside of my house. I should be glad, but I'm not. "Sure, I'll drive you by as we go home." I gather the consignment forms I'd piled on the table to look at, to gloat over, and the receipts for charity from Goodwill, and stuff them in my pocketbook. "Let's go now before traffic gets bad on the bridge."

Gerald must hear the tick of surprise in my voice. "We don't have to, Alicia. I just wanted to ask Betsy about something. I can do it. . ."

"No, I like to take care of things on my mind, and you do too, I see. And I'll stop by for groceries after I drop you off."

Back at the house, I settle the bags of groceries on the cabinet next to the refrigerator and pour myself a glass of wine. I am confused. Why am I so disappointed? We have had a good day. The look on Gerald's face when he understood that I am not angry at him for poking through the jewelry box was worth forgiving him. And he, in return, forgave me for finding his diary.

I take off my coat and go to the hall closet to hang it up. His door is open, his bed rumpled, as usual, a jacket hangs across the chair. Without thinking, I go in and straighten the bedclothes. And I wonder where he has hidden the diary holding the note from his mother, the one that made me his grandmother. It is not under the pillow.

The phone rings about the time I am thinking of calling Betsy to offer Gerald a ride. Gerald asks if he can stay for dinner there; they've ordered pizza and they are watching Grimm, "a TV show you wouldn't like, Alicia. I'm saving you a night of torture." He sounds happy.

I suppose I should be pleased for him. "Sure. When will you be home?" I'm beginning to sound maternal, but not controlling, I hope. I just want him to commit to coming home. To **our** home. My concept, maybe not his. And yes, besides hurt and worried, I'm also jealous of a real grandmother who knows to keep pizza at the ready. I suspect if I were to read a book on raising teenagers, I would be asked to describe my present state of mind as hurt, worried, jealous, beside the most important feeling that must keep a parent trying. I can't say that one aloud yet, even to myself about this red-headed cheerful boy.

Fred, on his death bed, punctured with tubes and filled with oxygen flowing through the fixture in his nose, wiggled a finger for me to come close to his lips. I leaned over him, my arms and hands overlapping his fragile body, and I felt his faint breath on my ear, heard the almost silent words. "It may not have seemed like it, but I always loved you in my own way." He coughed softly. "Thank you."

I could barely find my own voice as my lips closed in on his ear and I whispered, "I know, Fred." A shadow of a smile crossed his cheek. "And I love you, too, in my own way."

A day later he was dead. And I realized we were both telling the truth.

I've not found a reason to use that word since.

When the phone rings I'm hoping that Gerald has changed plans, is coming back soon. I hope I can stay awake long enough to open the door for him. Today's travels wore me out. "Hi," I chirp into the phone.

That rough voice is mushy like something rotten. "Hello, Mrs. Drummond. Is Gerald around?"

'No. What do you want?"

"Just tell him I'm trying to get ahold of him."

"Leave him alone. You are stalking him and if this continues, I will call the police." I hang up, but not before I hear him laugh.

A pathetic threat. I don't even know his last name, where he lives. Gerald doesn't either, I learn when he comes in and I tell him of Jake's phone message.

"He's just trying to jerk us around, Alicia. He's high, like always. He won't do a thing."

Our Monday breakfast of oatmeal and maple syrup will last through the morning for both of us, I'm sure. Oatmeal sticks to the ribs, my mother used to say when I objected to having to eat it in the morning before school. I say the same thing to Gerald as he pokes at it as if he doesn't know what it is. Maybe he doesn't. Can't get hot oatmeal in a cereal box, I suppose.

"Why?" he asks. "I'm okay with toast."

"We have a visitor coming this morning, remember? The man from the art gallery to look at what I have on my walls. I want you to hear what he has to say, too. It will be good to have two sets of ears and two kinds of questions for him to answer." I am wary of experts I don't know. Too easy to get taken, even when I am familiar with the possible value of the some of the pieces. "Ask him why something is worth what he says it is. It's okay to sound a little dumb."

"So that's my job? To sound dumb? Won't be hard." Gerald is drinking rice milk from the bowl he holds to his mouth. He likes hot oatmeal, it seems. "I'll even take notes."

We have the dishes cleared when the doorbell sounds. Like Gerald, John Mitchell also has a notepad in hand. We walk through the rooms and he does not mention values, only his appreciation of what he is looking at. He takes notes. Gerald asks questions and he is good at sounding a little dumb. Actually, he is, about art. "Why is it called a wood block print when it's on paper?" In front of a Dali print, "What is this supposed to be?" When we get to the oil painting, though, the road through the forest, he doesn't ask anything. He steps back and looks at it, his face solemn.

"Very nice," Mr. Mitchell says. "I can see that it speaks to you. Me, too."

Gerald does not take his eyes from the long road. "Do you really want to sell it, Alicia?"

I am surprised by his question. For a moment, I don't know. Then I remember what my plan is, to simplify my life, to find for a school for the boy who has come into my uncomplicated life and brought oatmeal and many other things back into my consciousness. The painting is part of the plan. "Yes, I'm sure."

When we've made the rounds of the art, the expert looks at his notes tells me that at auction the collection could bring thirty to forty thousand dollars, probably more. He'd like to bring the art to his gallery this week, write the catalogue, and get publicity out before the month is out. He gives me the details. "Are you ready to do this, Mrs. Drummond?" he asks as he takes out what must be a contract.

Gerald is looking out a window, absent from this discussion. His eyes don't meet mine when he turns away from the rainy view of the backyard. He waits for me to answer the question. "I'll let you know tomorrow, Mr. Mitchell. I'll call before noon."

As the door closes, I can't help asking, "What's wrong?"

He shrugs. "I kind of like the road picture. I'll miss it." He goes into his room and I find him lying on his bed, his arm over his eyes. "Forget it," he says when he sees me at the door. "It doesn't matter."

I remember saying those words to my father once. A boy I had a crush on, without warning, asked me to go to a party. There would be dancing and music and most of the kids from the clique that ran the school would be there. He'd drive me. I couldn't believe that this was happening to me, an outsider always too quiet and too smart for the popular group, no matter how often I smiled at them. When I told my parents, my father asked who the boy was. "One of those rich kids from Sumpter Street?" I nodded, and he said that he'd heard wild things about the goings on at parties in that neighborhood. "I'm friends with the school superintendent. He knows all about those parties. You're not going."

And I knew my schoolteacher father would not let me go no matter how I argued. "It doesn't matter," I lied. I opened my book bag, got out my homework. But it did matter. I remained quiet and smart and unpopular, and then chose a college far away from my parents. I went to parties, too many parties, felt popular for a few years, and then married Fred. I still wonder occasionally what happened to the boy who asked me to the party. And there have been times I've wondered what happened to that quiet young girl.

"I think it does matter, Gerald. We can leave the painting out of the collection when and if Mr. Mitchell comes to pick the others up. I'll tell him that when I call to arrange things tomorrow morning."

"Okay," he says. His arm remains over his eyes.

15

GERALD

Alicia was on the phone talking to someone about antique vases or something when Gerald heard a sound at the window. He could see Jake was crouched behind the lilac bush, pointing toward the park and at his watch. Ten minutes, Jake signaled with his ten fingers. He slipped away through the backyard gate and headed down the alley. Was he ready to give Jake the list of things he'd found in the house? No, but he had to.

He'd hidden it in his dresser drawer and he read it one more time. Mostly things Alicia said she didn't want anymore. Didn't seem so bad when he thought of the list that way. House cleaning, sort of. Alicia was trying to sell some of it right at this moment, wasn't she? Besides, giving Jake the list would get Gerald and Regan (if she still wanted to be a part of this "adventure") a couple more days to find another way to make Jake abandon his plan. Maybe they could get him arrested for pimping or scare him out of town. Or something. He put the paper in his pants pocket and called, "Going for a quick walk, back in ten," to Alicia who waved and kept talking on the phone.

Jake was waiting at the bench, his crooked smirk as evil as ever. Gerald could see what attracted Regan to him—somehow lately he had managed find ways to clean up. Most of him, anyway. The holes in his jeans still showed grimy skin.

"Like it?" he asked, holding up his arm to show a new jacket. "I got lucky. Found a place in the downtown shelter the city built for the likes of me. Social workers rescuing us poor teenagers. Toilet, shower, bed. I could learn to enjoy living like that." He pointed at the seat next to him.

Gerald sat down. "And the rules of that place don't include avoiding drugs and crime?"

"What they don't know won't hurt me. What do you have for me, Moon? I've been patient until right now. Gimme." His narrowed eyes carried a silent threat.

"What you asked for, in return for you disappearing from my life. Right?"

"No problem. When I get the goods from Mrs. Drummond, I'm out of here. Too rainy. LA awaits or maybe San Francisco." Jake held out his hand, flashed clean fingernails at him.

Gerald took the list out of his pocket and handed it to Jake who glanced at it. "No safe?"

"Not that I could find. I think she goes to the bank when she shops because she usually has cash. You'll need help to get all this out to the truck and maybe some boxes to make it easier."

"Dougster is ready. I told him Friday morning, show up here when you phone me that it's all clear. She is leaving on Friday, right? And you'll have the keys and alarm combination for me? "

Gerald nodded. "I'll be at Regan's and you can come by. I'll tell Alicia to lock up because we'll be off to a movie or something during the day." The plan was getting complicated. House keys, combination, and timing.

"And car keys. That Subaru is the best thing on this list." Jake glanced at the list in his hand. "The rest of it is mostly shit as far as I'm concerned. Dougster knows a few dealers willing to work with us and a pawn shop that will be interested in the jewelry and silver and maybe the fur coat. Not sure about the art. EBay maybe. I'll ask him. He's sold stuff he's picked up on the internet." Jake's eyes crinkled in a squint-grin. "Smoke?" he asked, holding out a joint.

"Car keys are next to the door in the kitchen. I need to get back before Alicia gets worried. I'll call Friday morning on your cell phone. You do have a cell phone?"

Jake handed him a corner of the paper, his phone number scribbled on it. "Regan gonna be around?"

"You'll have to ask her. I don't keep track of her." He'll warn her again about Jake's interest. Regan wanted an adventure and she might get more of it than she expects.

"I'll be waiting. Don't disappoint me." Jake pointed a finger at him and sauntered away from the bench into the park, his shoulders hunched as he lit up. Gerald got up off the bench and wondered if his shaky legs could make it back to Alicia's.

Alicia was still on the phone when he walked in. "Klawswani," he heard her say. "Yes, five pieces, both Japanese and Chinese. My husband collected them. I found the receipts in a folder in his desk. I don't know much about Klawswani, but several seem to be antique and perhaps quite valuable." After a pause, she continued, "Dikki shippa, and Meiji, if I'm reading this correctly, celadon something, Sato enamel, one described as Butterfly Rose. "

Something she said got the person she was talking to excited. "Yes, I'll be here today if you'd like to come by. Two is fine. Thank you, Mr. Mirakota." She gave him her address and turned to Gerald. "Fred's vase collection seems to be quite valuable. I always hated dusting those things."

"Klawsawni?"

Alicia spelled the word: "Cloisonné. French for an art style that involves wires, glass, and enamels." She led Gerald into the living room and to the vases on the buffet, one or two flowered, another covered with angles and straight lines, one with flying butterflies, all of them in brilliant colors. Metal strips controlled the blues and reds and greens like the black lines Gerald used to try to stay between, back when he had crayons. "Fred liked the old vases, but most of his are rather modern."

Gerald could understand why Fred liked these vases. He could imagine wanting to gather beautiful things just like these if he had the money.

Alicia looked around the room. "Most of the art on the walls were Fred's choices. And he loved music. He listened to it constantly. I've stored boxes of his vinyl records in the garage. Don't know what to do with them. I hear they are getting to be valuable. I wouldn't know; I can hardly play them now. Our good phonograph hasn't worked in years. I have an old one I sometimes plug in when I get nostalgic."

"He must have been interesting." Gerald wanted to hear more about him.

Alicia took his arm. "Let's have lunch. I'm tired of digging through old memories."

The cloisonné man showed up just as they were putting the dishes in the washer and Alicia hurried to answer the door. She seemed nervous as she called out, "Coming, Mr. Marikota," her voice almost a whisper. It must be hard to sell old vases filled with memories. She'd never talked much about Fred, what he was like, why they didn't have children, only that he liked art and bought a lot of it. Alicia wasn't attached to the things he admired, Gerald guessed. Maybe she wasn't attached to Fred anymore either after twenty years. Gerald wouldn't know about being attached to anyone, except when he was a kid and knew his mother loved him at times. Gerald was sure he loved her, too, once.

Gerald had no vases to remind him, just a diary with a lot of empty pages. And a note that lied to him. Every time he thought about his mother, a strap tightened around his chest. He tried not to think about her often, except when he couldn't help it, like right now. Maybe what he was feeling was one way of being attached.

Gerald closed the washer door, wandered into the dining room and almost bumped into a small Japanese man who held the butterflied vase in his hands. "Yes," he said. "Very nice. I have a buyer for this one." He gently placed it back on the buffet and picked up the next vase, the one Gerald liked best, transparent, the one that a person could see through. "Again, very special."

Gerald waved at Alicia as he passed by and pointed at the

hallway and his bedroom door. Alicia nodded. Maybe when her lips twitched she wasn't nervous but just sad. Cartons filled with carefully wrapped objects trailed behind Mr. Marikota when he opened his trunk and carefully placed them inside.

An hour later, a rental truck pulled up in front of the garage and the art auctioneer stepped out and crossed the lawn to the door. When Alicia opened it, he extended a hand and she took it briefly. "Come in, Mr. Mitchell. Before we begin, I have a few changes to our contract and if that causes a problem, we'll have to talk about it." Gerald saw that Alicia was wearing her strict, unsmiling face.

"Of course, Mrs. Drummond. What's the problem?"

She led him to a chair in the living room and took out her copy of the contract.

"I do not want to consign several of these pieces. I've thought it over, and these two are too precious to me to ...

"Of course. Which paintings are you referring to?"

"The oil by William Harrison. Of the road winding through the forest."

Mr. Mitchell looked at Gerald. "I think I know why."

"And this one." Alicia pointed at a painting Gerald had hardly noticed, a strange one, musicians playing horns and drums and a piano, none of them looking normal, more like cartoons. They were having a good time, their eyes looking far away into the music they were making. Gerald wasn't sure whether they wanted him to laugh at them or join them in their ecstasy.

"San Francisco," Alicia said. "A jazz club. Music that soaked into your soul, took you into unknown places full of sadness, love, joy, and crazy people."

"Helped if the listener was on whatever the musicians were using, didn't it? I remember the 1960's clubs. MJQ, Purple Onion, Hungry I..." Mr. Mitchell smiled and then returned to the picture and to Alicia's nod.

"I don't want to forget those days when I get old, really old. I'm going to keep this one, too. Is that okay?"

"Of course. If you ever change your mind, call me. In the meantime, let's get the rest of your pieces ready." Mr. Mitchell opened the door and waved to a man sitting in the truck. Between the two of them, the pictures were wrapped and ready to be taken to the auction house. An hour later, the truck drove away.

Alicia slumped in the maroon armchair in the living room, her eyes closed.

"Are you okay?"

"Yes. I'm just taking a moment to listen." She opened her eyes and looked at the painting of the musicians. "I'm reminded how much I loved jazz and the sound of the City. And you might spend a moment thinking about the road through the forest, what it means. It is yours, you know, for when you have a place to hang it and appreciate it even more"

Gerald was thinking about a nearer future, the day after tomorrow, in fact, and how he would explain the empty walls to Jake. Too hard to get rid of, he'd explain, so when Alicia decided to send them to the dealer to be evaluated and maybe sold, he didn't try to talk her out of it.

"Oh, I forgot to tell you, an antique dealer is also coming by this afternoon."

"Why?"

"I decided that the silver pieces just clutter my shelves. I don't care anymore about things that need to be polished and displayed."

Gerald remembered that one of his chores was supposed to clean the silver in the buffet. Both he and Alicia had abandoned that plan in the days they had spent in the rest of the house. Alicia opened the buffet cupboard, took out a teapot, pulled off the cloth that covered it and pointed at a fog of gray stains on its belly. "Tarnish. Obviously, I have not cared for years. No one cares any more about silver, a display of bygone times. Probably not worth much unless the dealer likes it because it's antique and sterling."

"I bet it used to be beautiful'

"It was, when it was used for receptions and teas and formal dinners, the kind of entertaining young women used to dream of in the Fifties. After the war was over, we thought we could return to life as it once was. Never happened." Alicia put the pot back in the cupboard.

"What changed?"

"We all did. The men came home from war, ready to get to work and find a life, but their wives had run things for the years they were gone, had worked, raised the kids, found out what it was like to taste a little freedom. Tea parties and silver platters and Rosenthal china like mine were still popular for a few years, but as more women returned to work, those things landed mostly in the buffet cabinets waiting for the next generation to put them to use. But it never happened." Alicia pushed past the swinging door and into the kitchen. "Speaking of tea, let's have a cup while we wait for the next visitor."

They were rinsing out the cups, mugs not china, in the sink when they heard the doorbell. Then Gerald followed as Alicia pointed at the glasses, tall, short, and fat and skinny in the corner cabinet. Gerald had never noticed them. "I see. Heisey. Twelve goblets, ten sherbets." Mr. Shapiro jotted a few words in his notebook. "Plantation blown. You took good care of these, Mrs. Drummond." His eager eyes lit up. "What else do you have?"

Alicia showed him the china, stacked and covered with felt. "Twelve settings," she said. "I've replaced the pieces that were broken over the years."

"Birds on Trees." Mr. Shapiro examined several plates. "Haven't seen this pattern in years. A few plates are faded. Dishwasher?"

"I had a careless maid for a while. I fired her and rescued most of them."

"What else?"

She brought out the tarnished tea set, platters, sugar bowls, and other pieces hidden in drawers and shelves, and the dealer copied down whatever he was finding on their bottoms, hallmarks he called them. Occasionally, he added an "Ah ha!" When he left, his notes tucked in his briefcase, he handed Alicia a piece of paper. She looked at it and said, "Add $250 to this estimate and it's all yours. When can you pick these things up? I'm not here on Friday."

"I'll come by tomorrow morning if that's convenient." Mr. Shapiro took both Alicia's and Gerald's hands. "Great doing business with you, Mrs. Drummond. See you at ten sharp."

Alicia looked pleased as she turned to Gerald and told him to sit down with her on the couch for a minute. "It's time for you to go back to high school, Gerald. I don't want you to go anywhere near where you have gone before. Do you understand?"

"Me, neither."

"We will begin looking for a good private school next week. The money coming in from this cleaning out of my old debris will help pay your tuition at first. If you do well, that is, work hard, and I think you will, I'll continue to support your education. Don't look so scared. We're in this together, Gerald. Remember? I will enjoy watching you bloom,"

Gerald was suffocating in guilt. He was a traitor to someone who wasn't even his grandmother, just a nice woman who wanted to help him, for some strange reason. He mumbled a "whatever" over his shoulder as he headed to his room where he pressed a pillow over his head and swallowed until the pain in this throat went away. He knew that, along with the guilt, he was scared, really scared. Of Jake. Jake would have nothing to steal and he'd get revenge somehow.

16

ALICIA

F red brought back the vases from his trips to San Francisco. I don't know why. Perhaps to appease me. Perhaps to serve as souvenirs of his experiences in that city. At first, we never talked about them, the experiences or the vases. Mostly we lived quite separate lives, he busy with his business, I involved with the workings of an expanding pipe company. We had good moments, of course, with mutual friends, at the theater, vacations, even a few years of Rotary, both of us volunteering on charity projects. I believe that others saw us as a successful couple. When we finally accepted both our need for each other and the reality of our marriage, we settled into a companionable relationship. This mutual acceptance came after he revealed his San Francisco assignations, and I confessed to an affair and an abortion, and we understood that we were both damaged goods, lucky to have each other despite our imperfections.

And now a man has packed the vases in sturdy boxes and taken them away. I am surprised by the loss I feel as they disappear into someone else's life.

I read somewhere that older people need an hour of napping every day. Today I take that hour, beginning with yoga relaxation from my toes to my hair, one piece of me at a time. By the time I get to my ears, I am dozing, any intruding thoughts shut down by my silent commands to my eyebrows, forehead, and scalp. When I wake up the house is silent. What day is it? What am I scheduled to do this afternoon? I gather my day. It is Tuesday afternoon, perhaps time to do that shopping for clothes for Gerald. I push off the bed, stand for a moment, hear him talking, apparently on the phone. To Regan.

"It's almost all set. . . Friday, right after they leave. . .Then I'll come to your house and we can go together." I find Gerald in the kitchen in front of the open refrigerator door. "Any cheese?" he asks. "Oh, here it is."

"You're making plans for Friday? "

He glances at me, perhaps surprised I overheard him. "Oh, yeah. Regan has a friend who wants to go to see *Spectre* with us. We'll meet her at the and then find a pizza place and maybe. . . "

"Actually, I was going to invite you to go with me now to shop for new clothes, for you. Do you want to? We can do some looking around and save you a little time on Friday. And, I want to stop by the bank and pick up some cash for my little getaway. I suppose I could use my card for everything, but I like having some money in my purse."

I can tell by the eyes avoiding mine that he doesn't want to go. "Of course, I can give you your allowance, and you and your friends can go on your own. That might be more fun?"

Gerald grins. "I had planned to do some work for the allowance today, vacuuming up the stuff that man left on the floor in the dining room and cutting back the lilac bushes a little. I heard them rubbing against the house this morning. I should help more." He raises his arms, flexes like a boxer. "It feels good to be in a real house, to do a few chores, to . . ."

He doesn't finish the sentence, but I agree, wishing he would say "belong here. "

I know I've cash in my purse, but I'll need more. A couple of hundred to give to Gerald for clothes, at least. And for a haircut for his red mass that has become untamed after a few weeks of living with me. And some cash for emergencies. I'm not comfortable yet about lending him my Visa to use. I'm not even sure one is supposed to do that.

I leave him raking and clipping bushes and I drive to the bank. Then I stop at Whole Foods and buy a pound of mac and cheese and some fruit salad. He'll be hungry this evening.

He's sitting on the porch when I drive up, locked out again. I must remember to give him a key for emergencies if I'm going to keep the door locked most of the time.

I let him in and he washes up in his bathroom, the door to his room open.

"You won't be locked out any more," I say as I hand him my extra key. "Be careful with it. I'm told that some children hang their house keys on a chain around their necks. Might work for you too, since you don't always wear your backpack."

"Like a latch key kid." I'm not sure what he means, but why does he agree so quickly to the offer of a key? Why does he then hesitate and ask if he uses it, will the alarm go off? I have an instant vision of a midnight escape to meet with someone like that Jake, a return in in the dead of the night. Or maybe even wild child Regan. I am ashamed of myself, an old woman still suffering from paranoia at a time when her days are happier than they've been for years. I force myself to admit, "The alarm is only set at night."

"That's cool," he says.

Cool? Fred whispers.

Why do I sense an alarm going off at this moment? "Do keep it on a chain or pin it to your pocket, or something. Wouldn't want you to lose it."

But Gerald is outside again, the key in his pocket, the rake in his hands. I go to my room, shut the door, and take the screwdriver out of my vanity drawer. Since I've turned it recently, the screw comes out easily and I slip the envelope holding the $1,500 the bank clerk has lined up so neatly in separated denominations into the safe. I screw the duct cover on and set the screwdriver on top of my vanity. I'll need some of it Friday when I give Gerald his allowance and take my own spending money. What is left will be safe in its hiding place.

On Wednesday, Mr. Shapiro arrives and collects his loot, leaving me a check that makes it okay to have him walk away with part of my home. It hasn't been very painful, this dissemination of the objects that once I thought earmarked my life journey. I'm not sure where all this clearing out will take me. Surely not back to where it all began. I don't want to return to that naivety, to that young woman who thought she was in charge only to discover that no one is. Life had come willy-nilly, despite the plans I'd so carefully laid as I slept for the last time in my childhood bed the night before we were married: a good man; a couple of children, of course; a career when it was time to have one; a comfortable house; later, more money and the friends his and my success brought us. We'd retire early, travel, and spend money and time on philanthropic projects for which we'd be recognized—the library, perhaps, or maybe the homeless. We'd grow old gently with grandchildren coming for Christmas Eve. Not like my parents. Better.

It would have been a good life. Had life itself not wandered in.

Nowadays when a woman discovers she has married a gay man, she can leave him and he'll come out. They often remain friends. Both will find new partners. Their plans will be adjusted as they continue with each of their lives. Love, partners, careers, reorganized holidays and reorganized children, travel, retirement, all the rest. Usually.

I am abandoning the plan I'd created when I was twenty. It had seemed such a good plan, with china and crystal and silver, and music and passports, and a fire in the fireplace. Even though children didn't happen, most everything else was almost as I envisioned it. Except for certain loneliness, not part of the plan, the emptiness that I could not give words to. I was too young that night I lay dreaming to understand that I was leaving the intimacy of love out of those midnight dreams: the softness of another's fingers, the heat of an arm draped across breasts, breaths moving across an ear. I had taken those touchings for granted.

If not right away, soon, I told myself, once I understood what I was starved for.

Then, when I couldn't wait any longer, I took a lover, a banquet of breaths and touches. I understood what it felt to be satiated, content. Until banquet ended.

I've thought that I might have found the intimacy I was seeking if I had had that child. Instead I, we, filled our lives with the rest of the plan, all of which came to pass.

And now I'm selling the artifacts of that plan. And maybe investing the proceeds in a new, unexpected dream of a young man who believes he is my grandson. I wish he were.

17

GERALD

The phone rang. They were saying goodbye to Mr. Shapiro so Gerald answered and heard Regan's voice, whispering as usual. "We need to talk. Finalize the plans, Jake says."

"Jake? Is he with you?"

"He was. He's going to make sure Dougster is on board with the truck and we need to know when the grandmas will be leaving. And, we need to find a hair salon for us to waste a few hours in and be seen. Alibi, Jake says. He wants the house keys and anything else you've discovered that will be useful."

"You and I need to talk, for sure, Regan. And if he calls you, tell him we can meet him in the park at tonight at 7:30, when it's getting dark. I have other stuff to tell you this afternoon."

"I have stuff to tell you, too. That Jake is something else."

They agreed to meet for coffee in a couple hours and they hung up. Gerald had some thinking to do first.

Alicia was in her room, packing for her spa day by the time he got back, wondering out loud where her old bathing suits were. Gerald told her he was going to go over to Regan's to make plans for the day but he was really going for a long walk to try to figure things out first. Like how could he help rob Alicia's house and lie about it and still think he could live with her, accept her offer of a good school, pretend he was a rediscovered grandson that they both knew he wasn't. Gerald hadn't done anything but lie to this old woman from the very start. But at the very start he didn't know he was lying. He thought he was reaching for someone who might save his life.

Not that his life was worth much, now that he has messed it up even more. The men who paid for his body, the drugs he used to make it all okay in his head, didn't hurt anyone but himself. And no one cared, especially himself, until an old man took him into his tent and treated him like a good person, told him he could find a different life somewhere away from the camp. Before that, his mother thought she would help, too, with a name and a certificate. She wanted her son to escape the life she had led him into. She must have loved him a little.

Gerald needed to stop walking, get some coffee or something, try to find a way out of what the next day would bring. He slid into a booth in a bar and when the waitress asked to see his ID, Gerald told her he was just there for coffee, that he was feeling sick and needed to rest.

The tired woman looked at the wild red hair, the wet cheeks, and said, "I been there," and brought back a cup of coffee. "Just a few minutes, though, okay?"

Her kind words made his throat hurt and as the waitress dropped a couple of paper napkins on the table, she added, "Good luck, guy," She turned to a new customer at the counter and whispered, "Not too long."

What he had to do is stop lying to Alicia. The first lie, about being her grandson. Gerald needed to tell how his mother thought she could give her child a way out. Gerald could do that, explain about the name confusion on Google and how he did not notice the name on the old certificate, only that it seemed to support of a piece of his mother's complicated history.

The coffee was hot, hard to swallow. So was his next thought. He had to tell Alicia about his life under the overpass, the things that he did, and if he could, explain why. Then the third lie must be revealed, his connection with Jake and his part in his robbery of Alicia's house.

But was it possible that Alicia would not discover his connection with the robbery? That the whole thing could look like a break-in by strangers? That he could sympathize with Alicia and that Alicia would laugh when he said it was okay because Alicia wanted to simplify her life, which now included losing her car? Maybe. Gerald left a couple of dollars under his cup and said thank you to the waitress. He felt better.

A new thought slowed his steps. What would he do about Jake and the almost empty house? Jake would be furious, crazy with the kind of anger he knew Jake was capable of. Gerald had felt in his fingers on his body, his fist on his face.

Gerald stopped in front of a shoe store. Faded posters of once-shiny men's leather shoes slumped in the windows, a scotch-taped sign, **Sorry, Closed**, clung by one corner to the inside of the door's glass. A dent of an entryway, old mail scattered like tired refugees at its threshold, seemed a like a good place to pause, to reconsider. The beer bottles and wrappers clustered at his feet indicated others had thought so, too. He smelled urine, but he'd smelled it before in other abandoned places.

He had to tell Jake the truth. Tonight. So that he was prepared to not get what he wanted. He didn't like not getting what he wanted. And it wasn't only Gerald he'd punish. Regan, too, who didn't deserve to be hurt. She was only a bystander, a goofy girl who thought she could find some adventure in a prison of a town. She was Gerald's friend, he supposed he could call her that, and he had to protect her from Jake even though Regan didn't think she needed it.

Jake had to get something important tomorrow, not just the car which he planned to use to get out of town in and then abandon once he'd gotten rid of the rest of the stuff he's stolen—or would have stolen. What's left? Only the car and a few valueless pieces of silver the antique dealer didn't take. And the old table no one would want. And a couple of paintings.

Gerald wiped away some grime on the window and peered into the dark shop, its counter dusty and cash register's drawers half open as if it had been emptied in a hurry. He hoped the owner had retired to Tucson and never looked back.

He hadn't walked half a block before he knew he had to do it. He had to betray Alicia one more time if he were to appease Jake and save Regan and himself from being beaten up or worse. And maybe, maybe—no, he couldn't hope for anything more than that—especially finding a grandmother.

An hour later, Gerald and Regan agreed to meet at the park right away because he said they might have a problem.

"Sure." He could hear Regan smiling. "I'll bring a few supplies that will help us talk."

"Don't. I need you sober."

They settled on the rocks behind the bushes.

"Sure?" Reagan reached into her bag.

"Very sure. You, too." Gerald was annoyed at the grin his friend gave him, as if she thought this was a game they'd joke about when it was over. Jake was not going to be laughing, nor will she.

"Most of the stuff is gone from the house."

"What stuff?"

"All the stuff on the list, or just about all of it, the valuable stuff, the good silver, the art, the antique vases, everything. Alicia went on a clean-out binge, has given it to people who will try to sell it to collectors. The only thing that's left, really, is the car."

"Jake will be mad, I bet." Regan opened her bag again. "Have you told him?" She didn't seem to believe him.

"He'll be furious. He hurts people when he's furious. Listen and start thinking. What can we do?" Gerald watched as Regan took out a joint and lit it.

Inhaling, she squeezed out, "I haven't a clue. And this whole thing was not my idea. I can just not be here when he finds out."

"Won't work, Regan. Jake will get us both, bad. Here or not. He found me when I escaped from him, remember? He'll find you too. You've taken him by Betsy's house."

"You're beginning to scare me a little."

"Enough to help come up with an idea of what to do?" Gerald

had an idea, but he was not going to mention it until Regan came up with a few ideas herself.

"We could act shocked when he calls to ask me what the hell is up. I'm good at crying when I'm in trouble."

"He doesn't care about crying. I've seen others try it. Also, he doesn't respond to threats because he knows any threat we make will be hot air, like calling the police. He'll include us, make it all our fault, say we planned it. "

"Why would we have planned it?

"For drugs."

"Why **did** we plan it?"

"I wanted to keep my grandmother."

"Doesn't matter anymore, does it? Google doesn't lie." She leaned toward Gerald. "Toke?"

"Regan!"

"So, what's your idea? Kill him?"

She might be serious. "God, Regan."

She squinted at Gerald through a cloud of smoke and she giggled. Something else besides pot was in that cigarette.

"Did Jake give you that?" Gerald pointed at the butt Regan held between her thumb and finger. "Did he call it a cocoa puff?"

"Something like that. Why? I feel terrific."

Gerald reached for the smoke, like he wanted a drag. Regan handed it to him, and Gerald smashed it under his foot.

"You retard!" Regan grabbed his arm and Gerald shoved her back against the bench. His fist headed for Regan's neck, but instead it landed on her shoulder.

"Shit! Why'd you do that?"

Gerald was not sure whether the girl meant the smashed butt or the shoulder she rubbed. "You were smoking a joint that contains not only marijuana but cocaine, one of Jake's favorite combinations. Not helpful for getting us out of this mess." He looked into her whoozy eyes, and said, "Get a grip and listen. Or go home and suffer the consequences. And there will be some when Jake blows."

Regan sank against the bench back. "So, what? What do you propose, Mr. Smartass?"

Gerald was not sure if he should mention the money in the duct to Reagan. The girl was high; no telling what she'd do with the information. "I'm working on a way to get Jake some money so he'll be satisfied with the car and some cash. It's not for sure, so for your own safety, don't tell him, not a word, especially about the stuff not being in the house, until I work it all out. I'm guessing he'll be checking back with you sometime before long. Remind him 7:30 pm tonight, here, for final plans and to pick up the keys.

Regan seemed to be listening. "7:30, right."

"And don't fuck this all up by smoking another cocoa puff or anything else. You can celebrate when it's all over. I'll join you then." Or not. Twenty-four hours could bring a lot of changes.

18

ALISHA

've been sitting too long in my old maroon chair. It's time to start doing, I tell myself. Thinking too much tires a person out. The first thing I need to do is find a swim suit for the trip tomorrow. And maybe a pair of long pants and walking shoes if we want to do a little hiking. Do I still have hiking clothes? I open a dresser drawer and search for the pair of canvas trousers I remember buying for some outdoor trip years ago. I find them at the bottom of the drawer, folded over the bag with the handgun in it, the box of bullets hidden in it. The other items I need to get rid of, I think as I cover them with a t-shirt. I find the shoes in the garage closet, probably too dirty to wear in the house and then forgotten.

I scrape dried mud off the shoes with a weed puller and sweep up the mess. The yard debris can is almost full, mostly the clippings and leaves from Gerald's cleanup. I should bring the bin out to the curb. Pickup is this afternoon, if I remember correctly. I have the lid ready to set back on the container when I notice a white slip of paper under a faded lilac blossom. I'm not sure if paper is accepted for yard debris. Probably not. I reach in and pull it out. Two pieces, actually, folded into a lump.

Something makes me open the lump, place the torn papers next to each other, squint to read the messy writing. Gerald's loose penmanship, I'm sure. He has made a numbered list : I. silver table ware, (buffet in the dining room) 2. jewelry box (Alicia's room). . .

A list. For what reason?

I take the papers and go back into the house where I flatten them out against the table with my fingers and look again. Nothing is changed. Gerald has written a list of objects and where to find them in my house. Even Fred's vinyl records. And my car? Why? I can't breathe.

Because I know why.

He is planning to rob me. Not he. The list with its directions suggests someone else will do it. Jake.

I carry the papers to my bathroom, lean over the toilet and vomit yellow bile. The bitterness in my throat matches my thoughts. Once again, I have failed at being loved. Once again, I tell myself it doesn't matter. I lie down on my bed and shut my eyes. Once again, I realize that it does.

An hour later I sit up and if it weren't for the treachery the list reveals, I would laugh as I read it again. Almost everything on it is no longer in the house. Some serendipitous stroke of fate has turned me into an obsessive cleaner-outer. The thief, whoever it is, is in for a big disappointment if he imagines himself carting off bags of jewelry and silverware. The boxes of records are heavy and if there are any left after the visit this afternoon from RC Vinyls, they'll be a bitch to lift into a car. Likewise, the few pieces of art still hanging and the table saw and the antique table.

The oil painting of the road will have to go on the roof of whatever they will be driving, no doubt will damage it. I should have sold it. Would have served the greedy kid right. No, not greedy, *two-faced*.

It's possible to feel the hardening of one's heart. A hard heart extinguishes the need to weep and offers the strength for revenge, a familiar idea for me, a person who has had several reasons to want to pay back certain persons in her life. Once I found it easy to step over a disappointing love sprawled across the path in front of me and not look back. Not this time. I cannot step over the lies of an almost-loved fifteen-year-old boy. I will proceed with the hardened heart that makes it so difficult for me to weep at this moment. I will step on him, not over him.

19

GERALD

When Gerald looked into Alicia's room after dinner, he saw that she had laid out three swimsuits and was packing a small bag for her spa visit. He left the house, the TV blaring loudly, and ran down to the park. A familiar dark hump moved on the bench and then stood up as he approached.

"Keys, Gerald. That's all I need, and the combination to the alarm."

"Here is the front door key. The combination will not be necessary. Alicia doesn't use the alarm much, only if she is going to be out of town overnight, which is almost never. Like I said, the car keys are hanging by the kitchen door to the garage." Jake took a step toward the path, and Gerald added, "But wait. There's more, lots more."

"Yeah? Like what? Like diamonds in the cookie jar?"

"Something bad and something very good. Sit down."

Jakes lips curled into a snarl. Gerald had to talk fast. "Alicia got it into her head to clean up her house, to give away or sell most of her good stuff, the antiques, art, even the some of the old records in the garage."

Jake's hand whipped out; his fingernails slashed across Gerald's cheek. "You told her, right? You double-crossing queer, I ought to kill you."

"No, really, she did it all on her own." He tried not to turn from at Jake's raised fist and what he knew would come next. "I couldn't stop her. But I did learn about something that would be a lot easier than carrying out a pile of loot to a truck which the neighbors would notice and report to the cops."

Jake, leaned close, his fist pressing under Gerald's chin. "What?'

"I saw where she keeps her money. Lots of it, I think, hundreds at least, probably more."

Jake hadn't moved; his rank breath assaulted across Gerald's nostrils. "Where?"

"In a box in the heat duct in her bedroom. The register screws on. I watched her, through the bedroom window when I was raking in the back yard, and I saw the screwdriver still on her dresser this afternoon." The words made their ways through gasps of pain. His cheek, something else deep inside. He was selling out his almost-grandmother. To save his own skin. And he understood, as he told Jake of the secret safe, that Alicia would realize how Jake found out about it.

Jake drew a square in the dirt in front of the bench. "If this is the house, where is the bedroom, and put an X where the register is." Gerald's hands shook as he held a twig and he did as he was told. Jake got up, brushed off his knees. "Okay, if this works out, you'll never see me again. I'm off to California with Dougster tomorrow after this is finished. If you are lying, you'll pay big time, Pansy. You know that."

"I'm not lying, Jake. Leave the house key under the lilac bush by the window in case I need to get in after you're gone. And then you won't have to worry about keeping quiet about me. I'll be gone, too."

Gerald made his way back to the house. *Queer. Pansy. Traitor.*

20

ALICIA

I am dozing in a gray fog Thursday afternoon when I hear the door close softly. Gerald's presence dispels the grayness. I open my eyes. Then I close them again. I can't look at him; his red-rimmed eyes indicate drugs or something; maybe crying again, but I doubt it. I doubt he ever cries for real or feels the kind of pain I'm feeling right now. I want to scream at him, hit him, pull his frizzy red hair from his scalp. But I've decided to play out the little scene he has devised, be patient, allow a robbery to occur, or at least begin, and then spring the trap.

'Hi, Alicia!" he calls as he heads for the kitchen. "Coffee?"

"In the pot. Still hot."

"Want a cup? Or do you have your tea?"

How can he sound so cheerful? I am choking on my angry thoughts. As he refills my cup, I ask, "What have you been up to? Have you had any lunch?" I feel my lips curve only at the ends, my teeth hold my face still.

"Walking. And Alicia, I need to tell you something even though it may change your plans about me, about school, about who I am." Gerald pulls his legs up under him on the couch and he is careful to place his cup on a coaster.

I am stunned. Is he about to come clean, confess that he is planning to rob me? But now I have gotten rid of most of the things worth stealing, so the plan is off, and he feels. . .what, guilty?

Embarrassed? The tightness in my body eases a little. I can handle this confession. Not forgive it, of course, but I will send this person away with both of our consciences clean and my house my own again. I am sad that this month of revelations is coming to an end, but all good things come to an end.

Also bad things, Fred adds.

"Go on."

Gerald opens the diary. "I hid this in your black suit pocket after I realized you knew where I had kept it. I guess I wasn't ready to talk about why I showed up that night and knocked on your door. I stole this diary from my mother before I left her and went to live on my own. You and I have talked about it before, a little, how my mother, had a piece of paper with your name on it, how she told me that if anything happened to her, I should find you. Then I Googled you and found you.

"What you and I didn't know then was that tucked inside the book were two old official-looking papers. A 1947 birth certificate listing Sonja Dubrinski and Petro Drummond as Alice Drummond's parents, and an Adoption Certificate dated in June 1978, six years after Gretchen's birth, which tells how Gretchen, her birth mother Alice Drummond, became Jessie Grayson because the Graysons had adopted her.

"I thought I had it all figured out, that you were my grandmother even though you said you'd never had children. Google doesn't lie, I thought. But I knew you didn't either, at least I didn't think so. When I asked Regan to Google Alice Drummond one more time, she was more thorough than I could be at the library. They time you, thirty minutes, and I had to hurry and I believed I'd found you, like my mother wanted me to. Regan found out that Alice Drummond, born to Sonja Dubrinski and Petro Drummond, had a child named, at first Gretchen, then Jessie Grayson after she was adopted. Alice Drummond died ten years ago. Her only known relative, a cousin Fredrick Drummond, your husband I'm guessing, preceded her in death ten years before."

Gerald's palms cup his eyes. Then he lowers his hands and gives me a wet look. "So, you aren't my grandmother. I'm sorry I bothered you." He pulls his legs out from under him and rests his feet on the floor. "I guess that's all." He gets up, turns his back to me, wipes his hand on his pants.

I stand also, wanting to comfort him. But I don't. How can I? This kid is going to try to rob me tomorrow. I should be wondering if he has told me this story to soften me up or to distract me or to give himself a reason for destroying my trust. Why do I feel so sad?

Because you are, Fred whispers.

When Gerald looks back, he says, "I'll leave on Saturday. I need to make up my mind where to go first—and I don't want to spoil your and Betsy's day off. I'm glad you are friends."

This liar is smart. Still going to give his plan a try for whatever is left here in the house that is sellable for his friend Jake. Maybe just my car. Maybe that will be enough to set the trap. "I'm glad, too, Gerald. But you must have been disappointed when you learned all this." Gerald nods.

I wonder how I can hold such opposing feelings at the same time: sadness and anger. I need to move away from this moment. "We'll decide what's next for you when I get back and have had time to think."

Gerald's door is about to close as the phone rings. I let him answer it, and I hear him say he'd like to have a Coke with the caller. They need to talk "about what we will be doing while Betsy and Alicia are spa-ing," he adds when he realizes I can hear him.

He calls to me that the two of them will grab some pizza and make plans for tomorrow. "Don't bother with dinner, Alicia. And I won't be late."

I will not phone Betsy to tell her what I know about tomorrow's plans. She has her hands full of a real granddaughter who may be even more duplicitous than my faux grandson. I won't add to her worries.

It's only early afternoon, but I pour myself a glass of wine, wait for V C Vinyls to cart off what 78's they want from the garage, to and wonder what my life will be like without a teenager to stir things up, including my own senses of joy as well as dread.

I haven't had worn any one of these swim suits on in years. My body has changed drastically, not that I've gotten fatter, only redistributed. The one-piece navy suit will cover most of the slippage, and I'll take the spa robe I bought more than twenty years ago in Maui to wrap around me. I'm aware I'm obsessing about swimsuits because I can't bear to think of what else will happen tomorrow.

Since most of the valuables are no longer in the house, I will let the plan become the trap to capture the culprits. It won't be difficult. Once at the spa, I'll call the police and ask them to check the house for me. I'm suspicious of a certain young man who has been hanging around, talking with my grandson, etcetera. I am assuming the police will keep an eye on and survey the house, to stop whatever may be going on. I'm assuming this will happen while Gerald and Regan are getting haircuts, certainly no later than their lunch at the fancy restaurant.

What might go wrong? I don't want to think about it. I fuss over a bathing suit, holding it up to me against my elastic-waist trousers and t-shirt and try to remember when I wore it before, and if I will ever get it around the doughnut of fat circling at my waist. I don't dare to consider what will happen to Gerald, and to me, after tomorrow. I'm beginning to believe it has already happened.

Where is he? The TV is on but he's not watching it. Not in his room. The front door is slightly ajar. He's left, for Regan's? I call. Betsy tells me that Regan is in her room pouting about something again. "I'll be so glad to get away for a day," she adds. "When did teenagers get to be so hard to live with?" Then she must remember that I don't know much about teenagers and she adds, "Maybe it's just my teenager."

"No, the one in my house is problematic also. And missing. Is sneaking out a teenage phenomenon?" I am merely filling space with the question. I have other teenage problems to worry about, things I can't tell this naïve woman.

"A requirement of being fifteen, I think," Betsy laughs. "He'll be back. They have expensive haircut appointments tomorrow morning at my favorite salon, along with lunch and a movie before we get back and have to face reality again."

As we hang up, I hear Gerald come in. "Went for a walk," he calls and goes to the TV and changes the channels. I continue to pack my day bag.

An hour later, I get down on my knees, use the screwdriver to open the duct-safe. Gerald will need money for his spending haircut and I should probably carry cash for tips and lunch. I count out five twenties for Gerald and five for me. At least twenty more bills are stacked neatly, the way the bank gave them to me, face up and by denominations, waiting to go back into the box. Then, a chill raises the hairs on my arms.me, a cold wave of bleak suspicion. I look over my shoulder, but the door is closed. Not tonight, but is it possible that Gerald could have discovered the safe sometime earlier? I don't see how. I close the door when I open the vent, which isn't often until last week. When was the last time I opened it? A day ago. Gerald wasn't even in the house.

I get up off the floor, reach out to close the venetians over the window. The garden is lit by a full moon; light slips through the half-opened slats. And I can imagine a face looking back at me from the lilac bushes, into the room, as I worked the screwdriver. I am going nuts. I am sure of it now. Blinds shut, I close the envelope and tuck the pile of bills inside the bra cups of the navy swimsuit I've packed in my bag. Then I screw the register back in place.

Good thinking, Fred cheers.

I also consider ripping out a few wires of the car but I'm not that paranoid. I'd have to pay for the repairs if my suspicions proved false. Insurance will pay for a stolen car.

Again, good thinking, Alicia.

Once, when I was still angry with Fred for deceiving me about his sexual inclinations and the wanderings resulting from it, I considered revenge. I tried having an affair, and hurt only myself, and then, depressed, I decided to that I needed pay him back by outing him. In those days, being a homosexual was a death sentence career-wise unless one was an actor or an artist or maybe a discrete woman. Fred was a conservative businessman, on a number of boards, successful both moneywise and politically, as a member of the city planning commission. He wouldn't survive the disgrace.

I hired a private detective to get evidence of his extra-marital affairs. I wasn't sure what I'd do then, maybe an anonymous tip to the rumor rag in town or someone he competed with, but it soon became apparent that the only incriminating thing he did in town was to visit a few porno shops outside the city limits. As my sleuth commented when he collected his check from me, "And that's not so unusual, you know. One out of two guys do it, even more often than your husband." He added, as he tucked the check into his shirt pocket, "But, with computers and TV coming in, men won't even have to leave their living rooms to get jollied."

I gave up on revenge and decided that I had to, and could, live with the man I'd married for better or for worse.

Our life ambled along through good times and not so good, like every marriage, I imagine, and I grew to appreciate his sense of humor and his intellect. And the gentle way he touched me to reassure me when I doubted his love. I grew to understand that I had a good marriage, only different than most. I was sad when he died, even though I bought myself a yellow sports car a few months later and drove it through that first year or two without him, graying hair flying in the cool Oregon breeze. Then I bought a Subaru and became a woman who had adjusted to being herself, by herself.

I apparently was thrown off track when Gerald appeared at my doorstep and started me moving in a direction that took me into places where I began to feel another kind of love, if I can call it that, for a child, an almost-grandson, a young boy who wanted to love me, too. Unknown territory. And ultimately, dangerous territory. A person could get hurt wandering here.

The revenge I've planned will not involve him, only his accomplice. He will be getting his hair cut or having lunch when it takes place. But it will be a lesson to him. And to me. He will escape a criminal record and because he is intelligent, perhaps decide to look to the social services for help and school. My lesson will reinforce what I've learned from my marriage. I must keep myself strong, not vulnerable, stoic, and content with what I can make of my own life.

I hear the front door close, his voice. "Alicia? You ready for tomorrow? I'll be back in a minute."

21

GERALD

Alicia was quiet at breakfast, her suitcase and purse waiting at the door. She nodded when Gerald asked her if she were excited about her trip with Betsy. "Of course," she said. "And you, are you excited about your day?"

Gerald had not been thinking about the appointment in the salon. He was not even sure what a salon was. He had other things on his mind. Not a sixty-dollar haircut, for sure. Short, he had already decided. And maybe a manicure, no color of course, but nails neatened up. "Do they do men's nails at this place?"

"Even toenails." She paused. "When I worked, my nails were colorless, polished with a buffer and cream, very businesslike, by a woman in my beauty shop. I did like having someone take care of me."

Gerald looked at his fingers, ragged, dirty even though he had washed his hands that morning. Being buffed sounded okay. To get ready for what comes next. The short hair was for that, too. Easier to keep no matter where he ended up.

He woke up that morning and knew that this would be the last breakfast he'd have in this house. No way could he face Alicia when his almost-grandma got back from her trip with Betsy. She might not figure it out right away, but Gerald's giving up the key, the secret safe, the car, was an unforgivable betrayal. Unforgivable because Gerald couldn't forgive himself for letting his fear of Jake destroy the only good thing in his life, ever.

He had laid awake most of the night understanding that he'd done it to himself. He could have been brave, talked about the awfulness of his life in the camp, watched Alicia's shocked eyes, listened to her disbelief, and waited to be kicked out. Gerald would have left disappointed but without hurting Alicia, before he knew how much he could hurt his almost-grandma.

He might have found another place to live, a shelter, or a camp with rules and protections. He had heard there were such places and even if there weren't, he would have survived somehow. He had been selfish. He wanted to keep what he was so close to getting. Just like Jake. Grabbing for whatever offered him an opportunity to escape the overpass, like himself, in a place where he had been convinced to sell Alicia's secrets rather than his own body.

Plans. Always plans for what comes next. Regan's friend Jane who unknowingly was to be a witness to confirm their activities that day, bagged out on them. That was one change. A second one was that Gerald decided he would leave Regan at Betsy's house after they ate lunch, no movie. He would say he was sick or something. He had to get back to Alicia's alone and get his pack and be hours away before Alicia returned to discover the robbery. Jake would be gone in Alicia's car, money in hand, minutes after he arrived. He'd want to get out fast, turn the car over to whoever will be paying him for it before Alicia could report it stolen.

He wondered when he would ever stop planning and just live. Not today.

After Alicia and Gerald ate a quick breakfast, Betsy knocked at the door and she and Regan came in excited for the day, but for different reasons. Alicia picked up her bag and asked Betsy if she had her phone, just in case something happened to either the grandmas or during the day. When Betsy patted her purse, Alicia turned to Gerald. "You've got the key to the house, right? You'll lock it when you two leave?"

"Sure, in my jacket pocket," Gerald answered. "We'll be okay, Alicia. Don't worry." He wanted to hug her. But he didn't. He just touched her arm and Alicia reached for Gerald's hand, brushed it as if she might like to hug him back. Instead she gave him a fold of money. Then she left with Betsy, and Gerald and Regan picked up the breakfast dishes.

'How much did she give you?"

"Enough."

"She must like you."

"I guess." Gerald couldn't say anything more. "Let's go." He turned the lock on the inside of the doorknob, and they started walking toward downtown.

"Are you worried—about today and Jake?" Gerald asked after a few minutes of silence.

Regan shrugged. "He said he'd be in and out fast; he even hinted he might drop by the restaurant where we're having lunch, let us know how it went. He asked me to phone him when we got there."

"Regan, he can't do that! He can't involve us in this thing. He just needs to get away, the way he planned. And we just need to do what we planned."

"I'd really like to see him one more time."

"That's so stupid. He'll be driving a stolen car, Alicia's car."

"He says he's already got it sold to some guy who'll sell it for parts or something. He's going to Alicia's around eleven and then come by the restaurant to say goodbye, and then deliver the car to the guy, who'll be waiting for it at one. Jake's got it all planned out." She gave him her rolled-eye look. "God, you worry too much, Gerald. No wonder. . ."

"No wonder what?"

"Well, you know—that Jake and you broke up. He said you were no fun after a while."

Gerald stopped and pinched Regan's arm, hard. "I told you that I left his camp and the street because he beat me up. There was no breaking up, there was only me running away from him before he hurt me even more. You can't believe. . ."

"He also said he saved you from prostituting yourself, fed you, let you sleep with him in his space. And that you left because you were sick, maybe syphilis he said, and that you wouldn't go to emergency because they'd send you to Juvie." Regan jerked away from Gerald's grasp. "I can't believe a thing you tell me. You lied to get into Alicia's house, didn't you?"

"Jake lies, Regan. None of that is true."

"Sure, Gerald."

"None of it," Gerald repeated. Regan turned and walked away.

He could run right now, take the haircut money and disappear. But if he did, Regan would tell Betsy about Jake and the overpass, and Betsy would tell Alicia, and she'd believe it. Gerald needed to get back to the house one more time, to leave the note he wrote to Alicia this morning, tape it next to the road picture if Jake didn't take it, let her know he would miss her. He had signed it "Love," and he was sure he meant it. At least, Alicia would find out one true thing about him, no matter what stories Regan spread.

"Look, let's just forget this conversation. After today, it won't make any difference. Jake will be gone, you'll be going home to your family in a couple of weeks, and Alicia and I will work out what's next, if anything." Gerald could almost believe what he was saying. Apparently, Regan did, too. She pointed to the La Belle Hair Salon.

"Let's go have some fun," she said. "We can fight later."

Like that time in the library john, it felt good to have someone wash his hair, massage his head, pull up the strands of red hair and say, "It's beautiful." Marge, his hair dresser, added, "Short is good. You have a good-shaped head for a curly cut. Here we go." An hour or so later, Gerald saw himself as he wanted to be: freckled, a redhead under control, and his mouth stretched into a smile. Even Regan was impressed. With the hair but not the uncolored nails.

"Why would a person do that, go pale, when you could do this?" she asked, flashing her rain-bowed fingertips at Gerald. "Grandma's paying, you know. You should have gone for it. Were you afraid it would look too hipster?"

Gerald wondered if that was the word she really wanted to use. "Where are we going now?"

"I made reservations at La Montmartre. French. Oo la la. I'm going to call Jake when we're done." She grinned. "I really want to see him one more time."

They have just been served a brown stew that smelled like heaven when Regan's phone rang. Her voice was a quiet hiss as she whispered, "I don't know what the shit you are talking about, Jake. Calm down!"

"What?" Gerald asked when Regan put her phone on the table.

"He said you had tricked him. There was no money. He and Dougster are going to trash the house looking for it."

Something had gone wrong. "Stay here, Regan, finish and pay the bill. I'm going to Alicia's and try to find out what happened. It would be better for you if you didn't show up. Play dumb in case we're fucked."

Gerald shoved his chair back and pushed his way out of the restaurant and down the street. A taxi came toward him and he waved the way people did in the movies. The cab stopped and he gave him Alicia's address. When they pulled up at the house, the meter read $4.50 and he added 50 cents for a tip that was received with a snarl. He didn't give a shit. Something awful was going on inside Alicia's house.

The front door was open. He heard yelling and thuds, and he found Jake and Dougster in the living room. The painting of the road hung crooked, slashed. Books cringed in piles on the floor, the bookshelves empty. Glass crunched under his feet. "Jake!"

"You come here, you lying faggot. I'll get you after I find that money."

"I told you where it was, Jake. In the bedroom duct. Did you look?" He turned to Gerald, his mouth an angry gash.

"The money was gone. What happened to it? Did you take it?"

Jake's familiar grasp of his upper arm signaled he'd get a fist in his face next. He turned his head. "Wait, Jake. I know every part of this house. If she changed the hiding place, I can find it. Let me help you." Jake didn't let go.

"Find it, or you'll be very sorry, Moon." They were back under the overpass. Gerald was back to his street name and the street game.

"First, the buffet." He pointed to the dining room. "She kept her valuable glass and silver there." He opened the cupboard of the buffet and Jake used his arm to clear the few contents left on the shelves. Glass crashed, and trays clanged as they landed on the floor. When the shelves were empty, Jake glared at him.

"Next?" He made the word sound dirty.

"Maybe the closet in her bedroom." He led the way to the room and saw the remains of the crushed duct safe, the plaster peeled off around the hole. Dougster tightened his arm around Gerald's neck while Jake pulled hangers from the racks and sweaters from the shelf, stumbling and kicking at the clothes scattered at his feet.

"Or the hall closet," he said.

"We've gone through that crap."

"Maybe the dresser." Gerald didn't want to suggest the dresser. If he were hiding something, it would be in the dresser, if he had one. But Jake began throwing the blankets and pillows off the bed. When he reached the bare mattress, he said, "Fuck this." He stood in front of Gerald and his fingers squeezed into chin and cheeks. "Where, Moon, where, if you want to live a long life."

"I said the dresser." Gerald pointed at the tall wooden chest of drawers against the wall.

"Too obvious." Dougster pulled open one drawer and then another and dumped their contents on the floor. In the third drawer, he slowed down and took out a black bag. "What's this?" He grinned, knowing what he'd found. He reached into the bag. His fingers wrapped around the barrel of a gun, a small gun, but a gun, and he held it up.

'Now we're getting somewhere." Jake took the weapon out of Dougster's hand and pointed it at Gerald.

"Fuck, it's not loaded. Dougster, find the ammunition. It's got to be close by." Gerald tried to move away, but Jake grabbed his arm again, the barrel resting on his temple. "See why people who cheat get so scared, Moon? This is for real, or will be when we find the bullets."

Dougster tossed out underwear, sweaters in plastic bags, and when he got to a drawer holding some bathing suits, he yelled, "Yes!" and held up a box.

Jake let go of Gerald and opened it. He took out the contents and held them in his palm like they were jewels. "45's. I've experienced one of these from the other side a while back." He opened the gun, shoved bullets into it, and clicked it shut. He turned to Gerald. "The money, Moon. Where is it?"

"I don't know, Jake. I really don't. The old lady must have gotten suspicious or more careful. Maybe she even took it to the bank. Maybe her desk has a record of it. In my—the other bedroom. The desk was locked and I never looked into it."

The front door banged. "Hello!" Regan's voice. "What a mess! Anyone here?"

"We're in the bedroom," Gerald called.

Jake's arm tightened around Gerald's neck. "Shit. Be quiet while I think what to do."

"She can help us. We still have the boxes in the garage to look through for the money."

Jake lowered the gun as Regan came through the door.

"What the fuck. . ."

"Your buddy here got his information wrong. We're not leaving until we find the cash. You, rich bitch, get to help." He let his captive go and slid the gun into the waist of his jeans. "Or not. Your choice."

When Regan reached out to touch Jake's arm, he jabbed an elbow into her chest. "Hey! Jake! I'm one of the good guys here. Remember? I'm going with you today, to San Francisco." She gave him a too-wide smile. "Aren't I? I've brought my Visa card like I promised. And I'm good at looking for stuff."

She could be under the overpass working a john, Gerald thought.

Jake ignored her. "How do we get into the garage?"

Gerald led them through the kitchen, opened the door, pointed at the boxes, some of them already open. "The old 78's," he said. "Might be worth something."

"Not unless the money's in one of them."

22

ALICIA

"Can't believe we're actually getting away!" Betsy turns the radio down, "Can you?" She glances at me when I don't answer her. "You okay?"

"Of course. Just took a little organization to leave Gerald and the house for a whole day. I'm doing a little breathing to calm down." My fingers tremble as I feel though my purse for the pink Pepto Bismo tablet I know is hiding somewhere. I find it and fuss with getting it out of its cellophane wrapper.

"Haven't seen one of those in years. Are you feeling sick?"

"Just a little stomach thing this morning. This will take care of it." I chew the dry wafer and swallow.

"I use Alka-Seltzer when I need something. Hell getting old, isn't it? Cataracts next, and a wonky hip that may need a shot or something. Our kids are so young they bounce back. . ." Betsy doesn't go on and I don't add anything about Gerald's health. I'm not sure I care. I'm not sure about anything except that the pink pill is part of my plan. We go along not talking for forty miles, the radio also silent. The rumble of the tires against the highway soothes me into mindless blur.

Then Betsy, with a sigh, breaks our silence. "I found another bag of marijuana in Regan's drawer in her bedroom." She doesn't wait for me to comment. "I don't know whether to tell her parents. I mean, pot isn't that dangerous, is it? It's legal here in Oregon for adults. Don't most teenagers try it?" Again, she doesn't seem to want my advice because she goes on. "She came to stay with me this summer against her will. I suppose she's angry, but she has been going to the class she had to make up, I checked, and she's passing."

"Good," I manage to say before she adds, "You know, she's not staying with me to make up the credit." The car slows a little as Betsy sends a glance my way. "She was two months pregnant when she arrived. Her parents arranged for an abortion, to take place after they left for Europe. I drove her to the clinic."

"That must have been difficult." A flash of a memory feeds my next words. "I imagine she was either angry or scared."

"She was neither. The next day she got up and wanted to go shopping. She has never said a word about it, except to thank me for the ride."

"She was relieved it was over. Over and forgotten. That's another ability we lose as we age. Memories lie like scatter rugs under our days, waiting to catch us off guard, to trip us up, send us spinning for a moment or moments." I'm not sure why I'm talking like this, waxing philosophical to a woman who seems so in control, if not of her granddaughter, at least of her life.

But Betsy surprises me. "You are right. I still go melancholic each year on my wedding date. I remember the few times we were truly married, like the day Regan's mother was born. Mark cried and so did I. Probably for different reasons, it turns out, since he had another baby coming with another woman. I just thought he was finally able to show his sensitive side. Three children later, the marriage died and so did Mark.

Something about the rhythm of the road, the world flowing by, the soft voice of the woman next to me telling me her secrets—something allows me to admit a truth I've never said to anyone before. "My husband was attracted to other males, even though he said he loved me. I believed him. Over time we developed our own definition of love, and I missed him in a quiet, sad way after he died." I'm sounding too maudlin. I add, "Of course, I mourned by buying a sports car and became a classic happy widow until I came to my senses."

"No anniversaries?"

"Only occasional regrets about exchanging my MG/TD for a Subaru."

Whatever barriers that had existed between us have been broken down by the telling of some of our secrets, and we talk and laugh our way to the resort nestled in the woods. I hesitate to say much about our mutual questioning of Gerald's sexuality until Betsy reveals that one of her daughters is a lesbian. We confess our uncertainty, how innocent we used to be about such things, and Betsy says, "The world's changed, Alicia, and I think I'm glad." I agree and we move on to our feelings about aging, and finally we get to the spa, all talked out. I've managed to set aside my plan until I take out the black bathing suit and the packet of bills falls into the suitcase bottom. We soak in a wooden tub and then it is 10:15; the kids' lunch reservations are at noon. I want to be home when it is all over, about 1:00, maybe. It is time to get sick, to make a call, to have to be driven home, to pick up the pieces of my former life.

"I'm so sorry, Betsy. I feel terrible, like maybe I have appendicitis. I can hardly breathe. Maybe someone here is heading back to the city so you can stay, I really don't think I should."

Betsy checks with the desk and learns that a bus full of women from the Sunset Retirement Center is leaving in a few minutes. I can make it to my house in a taxi from the center and yes, they have a seat, reluctant because I am sick but so is one other woman, they tell me. I am glad that I can leave Betsy to enjoy the massage and the green tea and a much-needed quiet time. "Is this really okay?" she asks, and she looks relieved when I promise I'll call her when I get home.

"Your cell number?" I ask. When she opens her purse to get a pencil and paper, she discovers her phone isn't in her purse, that she has left it at home, charging. That's the first thing that's gone wrong with my revenge.

The desk phone is surrounded by noisy women paying their bills. I cannot make the phone call I need to make once I find a way to escape from the spa and begin the two-hour journey home. The bus driver yells: "Last call for the bus," and it's too late to do any-thing but get on.

After a few solicitous inquiries from my seat neighbors, I pre-tend I am asleep and the other passengers also slump into silence. The bus is quiet for an hour except for two women up front who are asking innocuous questions of the bus driver. Flirting. They are easy to tune out. I go over my back-up plan to catch a traitor and his rot-ten friend who are at this moment robbing me. I hope the back-up plan works, a futile hope, perhaps.

The bus pulls off the road at a small restaurant. "Facilities here," the driver announces and his passengers groan and murmur "Thank Gods," some of them at least. I'm going to do something I couldn't do at the spa. The public phone booth is on one side of the entry, outside the restaurant, and under a shed roof, which is good be-cause it is raining now. I fumble with the change in my purse, find the note I've written to myself, and enough quarters to dial a desk at the city police department.

"Sergeant Oliver, Robbery. Can I help you?"

"Possibly." I give him my name and address. "I have reason to believe that a robbery may be taking place at my house. I am an hour away from town, and have just talked to a friend who said that when she drove by, my front door was open. She suggested that I have a police car go by and make sure everything is all right."

He repeats the address, then, after a moment, says, "Yes, some-thing is happening on that street. A security alarm has sounded; a car is on its way out to investigate. Where can we get in touch with you when we know what is going on?"

"I'm on the road, in a bus, and will be back in the city soon. I don't have a phone, but I will call you as soon as I get home."

"Ma'am, do not enter your home until you are notified that is safe. Call me when you are off the bus and near a phone. I'll know more then."

It may work. The old silent alarm on the kitchen door leading to the garage, separate from the alarm system in the rest of the house, has gone off at the police station. That was Plan #2, the shaky backup plan. Plan #1 was to have been a phone call from the spa to the station when I thought that my thieves would be in the house. Not much left for them to steal; a few boxes of records, several silver trays, a painting of a road too big to fit into the car, and Fred's dusty tools in the garage. However, it seemed probable that Jake would pack what he was taking in the car before he drove it away. That would take some time and he would have to go through the kitchen to the garage. If it still worked, and I had remembered the correct password to arm it, the old unused alarm would be set off. He might be in the house when the police arrive. I'll know in an hour.

I have trouble settling down for the last fifty miles of the trip, and I wish I'd brought something to read like my seat partner.

"I love thrillers," she offers when she notices me reading over her arm.

"Right now, I need something soothing to read."

She reaches into the bag at her feet and takes out a small book. "I've got just the thing," she says as she hands me *Mindfulness for Beginners*.

"Does it work when you are looking for mindlessness for a while?"

"I don't know," she admits, taking the book back. "I'm haven't read it yet. My daughter gave I to me, said it would help me to stop obsessing over everything." She chuckles. "I can't imagine a life with no obsessing." She goes back to her thriller and I have a feeling I'd like her if we ever have a chance to know each other.

The driver lets me out of the bus a few blocks from my house. I stand on the corner and wonder if I should walk in that direction and decide that since an hour has gone by, the excitement is probably all over. The streets are quiet. In a few minutes, I will learn if my revenge had been successful, if I have rid myself of a deceitful faux grandson and his buddy.

23

GERALD

Gerald took the car keys off the hook as he opened the door to the garage and pointed at the boxes of old records. "Might as well take them," he said. "Alicia said they are worth a little money."

"Money's worth money. Start looking in the rubbish cans over there against the wall. Dougster and I will load up the trunk with the records and some of these tools on the bench. Regan, help Moon go through the packing boxes at the rear of the car."

"What are we looking for?"

Gerald realized that Regan missed the reason for the trashing of the house. "A stack of bills about two inches high. In an envelope. I saw them from the bedroom window, but Alicia has moved them. They have to be here somewhere." Unless she somehow found out about the robbery Jake had planned. **They** had planned. But, how could she? The money was here somewhere.

Gerald dumped a bag of mulch, kicked over a stack of newspapers, stuck his hands into boxes that were filled with damp magazines and spiders.

"God, porn. Gay porn. Talk about weird." Regan held up a magazine cover of a smiling young man. "He's worked hard on his six pack. And his fingernails." Regan pointed to the hand spread below a bare belly. "Looks like yours, Gerald," she laughed.

Jake didn't look up. "Go to hell, cunt, and find that money before something bad happens to you."

The overturned boxes and containers revealed no packets of money, only a pile of decaying mice buried in torn newspaper scraps, cans of poison at their sides. After fifteen minutes kicking thorough debris and dead mice, Jake shut the trunk of the car with an angry bang. "This is ridiculous. We got to get out of here. Where's the door opener?"

"I haven't a clue. What does a door opener look like?" Gerald was telling the truth but Jake punched him anyway. He climbed into the driver's seat and inserted the key.

"Why would an old woman have this gay stuff?" Regan asked, her arms still in the box of magazines. "Probably over the steering wheel. That's where my parents keep it."

Jake pulled a metal box from behind the sunshade.

"Just push the button." Regan dropped the magazine and reached for the door handle on the passenger side. Jake turned the key and the motor responded. He aimed the box. The creaking garage door began to rise.

He turned, looked out the rearview window. "Holy shit!" He leaped out of the car and crouched behind the open car door. "I'm armed and ready to shoot," he yelled.

Gerald, kneeling beside Regan who huddled at his side, could see the gun wavering in the crack between the door and the frame. Dougster had thrown himself onto the greasy floor under the trunk of the car, his hands over ears. "Don't shoot," he called to whomever was listening.

"Place your weapon on the floor, your hands over your head, and come out of the garage." The policeman's amplified words made Gerald's ears ring. He raised his hands over his head and Regan whispered, "Don't do that. They'll think you're the one with the gun. They might shoot you, like on the news."

Jake yelled again. "I have a gun. I have captives. I will shoot them if you don't do what I say." Gerald, his cheek still stinging from Jake's fist, believed him.

"He won't, will he?" Regan whispered. "He likes me, he said."

"When Jake is mad, he'll do anything."

"I'm going to try." Regan got on her knees. "Jake," she murmured as she crawled toward the car "You don't need to be angry. We can get out of this. My dad has money. He'll..."

"Shut up." As he swung the gun in Regan's direction, his arm and his forehead, unprotected by the door, dissolved into bloody shreds behind a smoky blast. He doubled over, moaning, the gun, what was left of it, at his feet.

Gerald peed his pants, but no one seemed to notice as the officers rushed in, guns at the ready. They found Regan sobbing into her hands, Gerald scrunched behind a box, his wet jeans covered by a porn magazine, and Dougster between the back wheels of the Suburu moaning, "Had nuthin' to do with this. I was just passing by." And Jake curled next to the open car door, bloody, howling in pain.

The officers allowed an embarrassed Gerald and a stunned Regan, the "captives," to retreat to the bathroom and then the living room where they were questioned. After that, Jake was taken away in an ambulance, and Dougster, being held as a witness, left in a police car. Once the house had been searched, the officers said they had to wait until the owner arrived to find out what was missing. The teenagers could stay in the room that Gerald said was his bedroom. They had word that the owner was on her way.

"How could she be on her way?" Regan whispered. The grandmas' massages were scheduled for three o'clock and the spa was almost two hours away.

Gerald and Regan lay on the bed and twisted off the caps from a couple bottles of Kombucha which Regan had claimed was calming when she put them in the fridge that morning. Gerald took a swig, choked, and at that moment heard Alicia shout, screech actually, "I don't care if this is a crime scene. It is also my home, and I can see from where I stand that it has been desecrated. I need to go in and view what has gone on. And, even more important, I need to know what has happened to my grandson, who is supposed to be here."

Gerald heard a scuffle, a voice, "Oh, let her go in, she's no problem," and footsteps crackled through the debris.

"Old ladies are never a problem, right? Anything happened to Gerald, and you got a problem." Alicia again.

He called to his almost-grandmother, "I'm okay, Alicia. In my bedroom. Sounds like you need some Kombucha."

Alicia shoved her way through the door and past the officer standing next to her. And she burst into tears. Big tears. The kind one needs a towel and a shoulder to manage. Gerald threw a corner of the blanket across the front of himself. He was grabbed, held, wetted. By someone who wasn't his grandmother.

Regan watched them. She was crying, too. "You guys are so lucky," she said.

24

ALICIA

Two weeks later there's still some blood on the car door. I can't wash it off until the forensic team comes tomorrow, and so I spend my waiting time looking at Fred's porno materials. Some of the men are attractive, even to an older woman who hasn't given thought to such things for many years. When I've had enough excitement, I set the box out for the recycler who will come today. "We're moving on," I say to Gerald.

He has told me why he agreed to help Jake rob me. About the slow-roaming cars, Jake's hand reaching for dollars, and for him, and the cardboard bed, the kind old man who gave him the courage to leave the overpass, to look for a grandmother. I know about blackmail, or the threat of it. I understand how the threat of it made a good man lie about himself and kept a good woman standing by him. For what reason? Same reason. To keep a life going according to some kind of plan, if there was one. Gerald and I are seeing a counselor together to help us figure out the next plan.

I think you don't need me anymore, Alicia. Fred sounds relieved.

We have learned new vocabularies this month. Google, B&E, cunt, food with no eyes, *Pulp Fiction*, Cheetos, mindfulness (me, I've ordered the book), and STD, cloisonné, Kombucha (still in my fridge), wood block, courage (Gerald), and we've learned, maybe, some of the several meanings of the word love.

When it is over and I see that Gerald is all right and in fact, is smiling from his bedroom at me late that afternoon, I know what I feel and I can name it. And when he hands me a wrinkled note from his jeans pocket that reads *goodbye, love,* I am overwhelmed that the goodbye isn't real, but that the love is. I know that, because he kisses me as I open the slip of paper. And I kiss him in return.

Later Betsy calls, sounding lost and guilty. "What should I have done? Now Regan says she hates me, that she wishes she'd never met me. The only thing I did was let her parents know she had been involved with a young man she would have run away with had he not been arrested in the middle of a break-and-entering crime, and who almost blew his hand off firing an old, uncared for gun at her and a passel of cops."

I tell her, "You've done exactly what you should have. Sooner or later, Regan will understand. Love doesn't mean letting loose; it means hanging on, through thick and thin, and you have done that. She will know this when she gets over being angry at her small world and finds a larger one she's more comfortable in."

All at once, I've become a wise grandma.

Goodbye, dear, Fred calls from somewhere.

Today Gerald and I are taking the road painting to be repaired. Then next week, we are going to court. I am adopting him as my child. In a few months, he will be Gerald Drummond, son of Alicia Drummond. I will be his mother forever. His dead mother, the one who cared enough to hand him my name, will be glad, I'm sure.

THE END